Something was wrong.

The store was a mess. The glass teapot, the one he had noticed the day before, was on the floor, shattered into several pieces. Beside it on the floor was a bloody handprint.

It felt like the world was collapsing around him. He glanced back at Gwen. She didn't need to see this, but he couldn't keep her from the truth...or what they could possibly find if they went into the shop.

"Gwen," he said, turning around slowly to face her.

"What's wrong?" she asked, all the playfulness that she had been exuding disappearing.

He shrugged. "I can't be sure until I look."

"What do you want me to do?"

He could make her wait in the car, but whoever was gunning for her had to be someone they both knew, someone close to them, and it was likely it was someone who could lure her out of the car... and do whatever they deemed necessary.

He couldn't risk it.

MS. CALCULATION

DANICA WINTERS

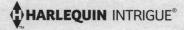
HARLEQUIN INTRIGUE®

To Mom

You show me what it means to be empowered.

I couldn't have done any of this without you.

ISBN-13: 978-0-373-75701-5

Ms. Calculation

Copyright © 2017 by Danica Winters

Recycling programs for this product may not exist in your area.

Printed in U.S.A.

Danica Winters is a multiple-award-winning, bestselling author who writes books that grip readers with their ability to drive emotion through suspense and occasionally a touch of magic. When she's not working, she can be found in the wilds of Montana, testing her patience while she tries to hone her skills at various crafts—quilting, pottery and painting are not her areas of expertise. She believes the cup is neither half-full nor half-empty, but it better be filled with wine. Visit her website at danicawinters.net.

Books by Danica Winters

Harlequin Intrigue

Mystery Christmas

Ms. Calculation

Smoke and Ashes
Dust Up with the Detective
Wild Montana

Visit the Author Profile page at Harlequin.com.

CAST OF CHARACTERS

Deputy Wyatt Fitzgerald—The finest (and sexiest) deputy in Mystery, Montana, who finds himself neck-deep in a murder investigation that calls into question not only his investigation skills, but a whole slew of his family's history. Wyatt had always hoped to find Gwen back in his life, but he never imagined it'd be under these circumstances.

Gwen Johansen—A no-nonsense cowgirl and Wyatt Fitzgerald's former high school girlfriend whom Wyatt's never quite gotten over. Though she equally loves and hates her family, when her sister turns up dead, Gwen will do whatever it takes to find the person responsible—even if the murderer is close to home.

Bianca Johansen—An angelic and unassuming small-town vet who is found murdered on Wyatt Fitzgerald's family's ranch, launching one of the hardest cases Wyatt will ever have to investigate.

Eloise Fitzgerald—Foster mother and caregiver not only to the people in her life, but to the animals, as well.

Alli Fitzgerald—The ex-wife of Wyatt's brother and head groundskeeper at Dunrovin Ranch.

Christina Bell—Alli's sister and Monica Poe's friend, who finds herself deep in the center of the conflict that is taking over the ranch.

Winnie Bell—A precocious little girl who loves taffy and everyone who works at the ranch.

William Poe—A shady county tax appraiser who thinks everyone and everything belongs to him—even the women of Mystery, Montana.

Monica Poe—The trophy wife who appears to be cooperating with Wyatt's investigation.

Carla Johansen—The town drunk who always seems to be at the wrong place at the wrong time, and who has a knack for taking things from bad to worse.

Prologue

There was nothing that could make a woman go crazy more quickly or more profoundly than a man. The same went for mares and studs, and the proof was the lame horse that had brought Bianca to Dunrovin Ranch in the little town of Mystery, Montana.

The paint had her rear end backed into the corner of her stall, an instinct to protect herself from predators who, if she'd been in the wild, would have already taken advantage of her injury and moved in for the kill.

Bianca snorted slightly at how the instincts between animals and people were the same. When everything was stripped away—the names, the relationships, the social frameworks and the money—humans were nothing more than animals.

According to Mrs. Fitz, the paint mare had

been in heat and had gotten into a fight with another mare when they'd turned the paint out. Normally the two mares had gotten along, their hierarchy and roles within their social group well established, but due to the proximity of a buckskin stallion, things had taken a turn for the worse and the mare had injured her foot in the fight. Bianca wasn't sure if the animal's leg was sprained or broken; she'd have to get her hands on the horse before she'd know.

"Hey, baby," Bianca cooed as she slowly opened the stall's door and moved in closer to the mare.

The horse gave a long huff as it looked over at her. It had the wide eyes of an animal in pain and it was breathing hard. Her left front leg was swollen and angry-looking, and from the state of it, it was easy to see why Mrs. Fitz had been upset when she'd called. If a horse broke a leg, which appeared to be the case here, it sadly often ended with the animal being euthanized.

It was the worst part of her job—making the choice between life and death.

In preparation for the worst, she'd already drawn up the syringe of Beuthanasia and left it in her bag just outside the stall in an attempt to keep from spooking the animal more than necessary. Though the recommended dose was two milliliters for every ten pounds, she'd doubled it. It was always better to have too much of the powerful anesthetic—it was more humane. One little prick of a needle and a squeeze and the numbness would wrap the animal's world in a shroud of darkness.

The mare moved to paw the ground in agitation, but as she shifted her weight, she stumbled and squealed in pain. The sound made the hairs on Bianca's arms rise. She personally knew all about pain—though hers was of the emotional kind. The kind no one noticed, until they looked deep in her eyes and then—fearing what they saw would catch—they turned away.

The whites of the mare's eyes were showing, her chest was flecked with saliva and sweat rolled down her coat. These were just more signs that what Bianca feared doing most may be just the thing she would be forced to do. She already hated herself for the choices she had made in her private life. This would only make her feel worse.

She watched the horse carefully as she approached with metered caution. A hurt animal was a dangerous thing.

"It's okay, girl," she whispered.

The mare threw her head and staggered as the motion forced her to catch her body weight on the injured leg.

"No, sweetheart, no, calm down." Bianca moved closer and gently ran her hand down the mare's leg. From touch alone, she couldn't feel a definite break.

Maybe she could save the animal after all. Some of the dread she'd been feeling drifted from her. Perhaps today, instead of taking a life, she could save one.

Bianca stood up and traced her fingers over the star on the mare's forehead. The horse's ears flicked to the right, like a finger pointing to something just over her shoulder.

Bianca turned to see what the animal was looking at. The person was small, but they moved fast.

The needle plunged into Bianca's neck. The anesthetic burned as they forced the syringe's contents into her.

Bianca's scream echoed through the stable as she grasped at the empty syringe that protruded from her skin. She fumbled with it, pulling it out and watching in horror as the needle fell onto the hay strewn at their feet.

Red boots… She recognized those horrible boots.

The darkness flooded in from all sides as the anesthetic pumped through her body.

She'd been right. More Beuthanasia *had* been better.

Death came quick.

Chapter One

Everyone in law enforcement would admit the worst aspect of the job was notifying the next of kin when a loved one died. Today that job fell on Wyatt Fitzgerald's shoulders... Well, not *fell* exactly, so much as it was a weight he'd offered to bear. The fact that they were only a few weeks away from Christmas only made it that much harder.

He parked his patrol unit at the end of the Johansens' driveway, as far from the front door as possible so he would have plenty of time before he would have to face them—and his former high school girlfriend, Gwen. The last time they had spoken, almost a decade ago, she'd made it clear she hated him. What he was about to do would only make her hatred for him worse, and he wouldn't be able to hold those feelings against her.

Though it was early in December, he was surprised they hadn't started to decorate for the holidays. When he'd been younger, they'd always had the Widow Maker Ranch decked out, complete with handmade pine-bough wreaths and thousands of lights. From the look of the derelict place, with its shabby siding and in-need-of-new-shingles roof, it was like the Johansens were just waiting for someone to arrive with news like his.

This moment, his coming to the door with the news of the death of their beloved sister and daughter, would be etched in their memories forever. And he would always be remembered as the catalyst for this tragic change in their lives. Without a doubt, they would always blame him for the hurt they were about to experience. In a way, he felt almost responsible for Bianca's mysterious death.

The snow crunched under his boots as he made the long march up the driveway to the ranch house's door. Maybe he should have brought along the other officer. They'd always been taught to go in pairs. It made it easier to face what had to be done. But this time, under all the extenuating circumstances, he felt this was one journey he had to make on his own—

that was, right up until the door was within his line of sight.

He would make it quick. Like a Band-Aid. One rip and it would all be over—at least for him. Then the real pain would begin for them. He cringed at the thought of how Bianca and Gwen's mother, Carla, would take the news. Ever since her husband's accident with the hay tedder at Dunrovin Ranch, she'd never been the same and she'd never forgiven his family or the crew that helped run the place. To her, everything about the accident had been Dunrovin's fault, and therefore its owners—Wyatt's parents—were to blame.

His stomach clenched as he realized this moment, his coming to the door with tragic news, was something Carla had gone through once before. Their shared past would amplify everything. He hated having to be a part of her pain once again.

He took a long breath in a failed attempt to calm his anxiety and knocked on the front door. The glass rattled as he tapped, loose thanks to the years of neglect since Mr. Johansen's death.

The last time Wyatt knocked on this door had been the night of their senior prom. If only he could go back in time to the days when his biggest worries were centered on how much playtime he would get in the Friday-night football game, and whether or not Gwen would be free to watch.

The curtain was drawn back and Carla's face appeared in the window. Her nose was red and purple and covered with the spider veins indicative of a long-term alcoholic—not that he could blame her after the life she had led. Her wind-burned skin, the mark of all serious ranchers, had more lines than he remembered and her hair had turned gray, but she still had the same dark eyes of a haunted woman.

"What the hell do you want? I'm fresh out of doughnuts," she said through the glass, her words slowed by booze even though it was early in the day.

"Mom, seriously?"

He recognized Gwen's voice and his heart picked up pace as she stepped into view. Some feelings really didn't change over ten years, no matter how much they should have.

Unlike her mother, Gwen was even more beautiful. Her long blond hair was haloed around her face, as wild as the woman it belonged to. She looked at him and her mouth opened in surprise, her hands moved to her hair and she tried to force it to submit. Pulling it back, her blue eyes picked up the bits of the morning sun, making them glow with life. Her eyes were just like Bianca's, reminding him of the death that had brought him here.

Gwen opened the door and stood in silence for a moment as she stared at him in his full uniform. Without saying hello, she turned to her mother. "What did you do last night?"

He shifted his weight, uncomfortable that she was chastising her mother in front of him like he wasn't even there.

Carla rubbed her nose drunkenly, like she was trying to process her daughter's accusation. "I wasn't doin' nothing."

"Then why is Deputy Fitzgerald standing on our doorstep?"

So they weren't on a first-name basis anymore. Apparently she wasn't feeling the effects of nostalgia like he was. He forced his feelings down. It didn't matter what she thought of him; that wasn't why he was here.

Carla looked at him and frowned as though replaying the events of last night through her mind. As he looked at her, he couldn't help but wonder if she was still drunk from the night before, or if the alcohol on her breath was just this morning's continuation of last night's party.

"I don't think I was driving." She leaned around him, looking out into the driveway for a car that wasn't there. "Bubba drove me home. I kinda remember…"

Gwen crossed her arms over her chest as she glared at her mother. "Are you kidding me? You don't even remember how you got home last night? This has to stop. It's only a matter of time until you're going to get into real trouble—" Her glare shifted to him as if she remembered exactly who he was. "So what did she do this time? How bad is it?"

The look on her face made him want to be standing anywhere but in her bull's-eye.

"Actually, I was here for—"

"Where's Bianca?" Carla interrupted, glancing behind her for her other daughter— a daughter who wasn't going to come.

"Mom, be quiet. Bianca will be along," Gwen said, moving between her mother and the door as if she was so embarrassed by her mother's ramblings she wanted to hide her from his view.

He cleared his throat, wishing he had loosened the top button of his uniform before he'd made his way to the door. Even his body armor felt tight, and he gave it a slight tug in an effort to dispel some of the discomfort he was aware wasn't really physical.

"Actually, I'm here about Bianca." As soon as the name fell from his lips, Gwen's scowl disappeared, replaced by a wide-eyed look of fear.

"She's upstairs," Gwen said, absently motioning toward the wooden staircase that led to the second floor of the ranch house. "Do you want me to go get her up?" There was an edge to her voice, a sharpness that came with panic.

He moved to touch her, but stopped and gripped his hands together in front of him to keep his body and emotions under control.

"I'm afraid to tell you this, Ms. Johansen," he said, moving slightly so he could look the older woman in the face as well. "Mrs. Johansen. I'm sorry, but in the early morning hours, we found Bianca's body. She is…deceased."

He knew he should have just said *dead*, but he couldn't get the word past his lips. It was too harsh for Bianca, the veterinarian who'd been a regular at Dunrovin. He'd seen her so many times over the years, and they had a friendship based on their mutual attachment to animals—and her sister. In fact, Bianca had been kind to him, offering him tidbits about Gwen's life and her dating status, and once in a while pushing him to make his move to get her back. But he'd always brushed away Bianca's urging. He and Gwen had already had their chance—he couldn't go through that kind of heartbreak. It nearly broke him once. He couldn't risk something that raw again.

"Deceased?" Gwen said the word as though she tasted its full, bitter flavor and spat it out.

He wanted to look down at the ground, to escape that gaze of hers that made every part of him charge to life. "Yes. I'm so very sorry for your loss."

Carla stared at him and blinked, the action slow and deliberate. "No."

Gwen's hand slid down the door with a loud squeak, like nails on a chalkboard…but he knew what the sound really was—it was the sound of a heart breaking.

She collapsed on the floor, her head hitting the wood with a thump so loud he rushed to her side to make sure she was still conscious.

"Gwen… Gwen, are you okay?" He touched her face and looked into her eyes. They were filled with tears, tears that wet his hand as they dripped over his skin and fell to the floor. There wasn't blood or a bruise where her head had hit the ground, but she wasn't okay. She wasn't going to be okay for a long time.

He stroked away her tears as she lay on the floor and cried. Her body was riddled with sobs, hard and heavy.

He wanted to tell her everything was going to be all right. That she would get through this. Yet he couldn't bring himself to lie.

Some people held the belief that time healed all pain, but he knew all too well it wasn't true. All time did was push it further from the mind, but just like a deep flesh wound, any time he brushed the area the pain was just as all-consuming and powerful as when the blow first struck. That cliché about the healing power of time was for the weak—for the ones who couldn't face the reality of a future filled with wounds that wouldn't heal.

Regardless of the state Gwen was in, he knew how strong she was. How much it took to bring her to this point. And he'd been the one to break her.

He hated himself.

"Shh…" he said, trying to calm her and help her in the only way he knew how.

Carla opened the door wider and stepped by him and out into the crisp morning air. "Not again…"

Gwen looked at her mother and, moving his hand aside, she rubbed the tears from her face and took a series of long breaths. "I'm fine… I'm fine…" she said, as though she was trying to convince herself. She sat up and smoothed back her hair.

Wyatt stepped out of her way and tried to ignore his feelings of rejection at her pushing him away. "Currently, Bianca's body is at the crime lab. As her death was unattended, she will need to undergo an autopsy in order for us to generate a full report."

Carla hugged herself as she rocked back and forth. Gwen stood up, and, brushing off her red plaid nightgown, she stepped to her mother's side and wrapped her arm around Carla's shoulders. "It's okay, Mom. It'll be okay."

At least one of them had the strength to feed Carla the lines she needed to hear.

Gwen looked at him, her eyes red and thick with restrained tears. "A full report? What does that mean? You don't know how she died?"

He shook his head. "The coroner was unable to make a determination as to the cause of death. It will need to be fully investigated by the medical examiner."

She frowned and her gaze flicked to the right as though she was remembering something. She opened her mouth to speak, but stopped, and then after a moment started again. "Where did you find her?"

The discomfort he had been feeling amplified. "She was found in the stables of the Dunrovin Ranch."

"Your family's place? Again?" Gwen asked, like she was calling him out for somehow being party to her sister's death.

He nodded, guilt rising in him as her poorly veiled accusation struck. "One of my mother's mares had come up lame. Last night, Bianca came to assess the animal and determine a course of treatment. We found Bianca's body at about 1:00 a.m. From our estimates she had been dead for at least an hour."

"No one found her until then?" Gwen's voice rang with disgust. "How is that possible? You have more hands and staff than most working ranches. Someone had to have found her before then."

He heard the slam at the fact that his family's place was merely a guest ranch and not a working cattle ranch like theirs. Her words were flecked with pain, anger and denial—whatever she said now couldn't be held against her.

"I don't know the ranch's current schedule. I've been out of that world, or at least a casual bystander, ever since I went to work for the department." He realized he was answering her and defending himself against her allegations when all he should have been doing was being compassionate and taking the verbal hits she chose to let fly.

"You're a bastard," Carla spat out. "You and your dang family. You're a scourge on the valley. You are the reason…you're the reason my daughter's gone. And now you tell me you don't know how she died. You're about as good at police work as your family is at ranching."

Gwen sucked in an audible breath at the sting of her mother's lashes. "Mother, stop." She let go of her mother's shoulders, repulsed.

Carla pointed at him with an unsteady finger. "You can't tell me I'm wrong. He is doing a piss-poor job. How dare he come here without answers. If he was a real cop, he'd be able to tell us what we need to know. He'd be able to tell us about Bianca."

It was as though her mother's words had pulled Gwen back from the platform of anger she'd been standing on a moment before, a platform that had been targeted at him.

She looked at him with a mix of pity and pain. "Don't say that, Mom. Just go inside. Go to bed and sleep off the booze."

Carla shook her head, but staggered inside and toward her bedroom at the back of the house.

Gwen leaned against the porch's white railing. "Did she commit suicide?" she asked, the question coming out of nowhere...almost as though she knew something he didn't.

"Right now we believe that may be so, but we are unsure as to the cause of death—we'll have to wait on the results of her autopsy. But may I ask if you believe Bianca had motive to kill herself?" he asked, wondering if Gwen knew something that would help him make sense of Bianca's death.

She shrugged. "Vets have high rates of suicide—more than a lot of other professions." She said it like it was just another fact from a book she read and had nothing to do with her reality.

"Was she having some mental health issues? Issues you believe would have led to her taking her own life?"

Gwen sighed. "She's been unhappy, and

with the holidays coming up… But I don't think she'd have the power to do something like that. She wouldn't." She shook her head, like she could shake the idea from her mind.

But now the cat was out of the bag and there was no going back. His investigation had just moved from what some had assumed was a natural death to something else entirely. Why would a woman like Bianca, who had a family who loved her and a mother who clearly needed her, be that unhappy—was it her mother's drinking, or something more? What had been going on in her life?

His gut twisted with a nagging feeling that everything wasn't as it seemed—and that his life, as well as Gwen's, was about to get turned upside down.

Chapter Two

She couldn't even look Wyatt in the eyes. Why did *he* have to be involved with the investigation of her sister's death? There had to be at least a dozen other guys on the force who could have stepped in on this one—at least to notify Gwen and her mother of the death. Yet, there he stood…with his broad shoulders, honey-colored skin, scruffy jaw and those cheekbones, all of which often found their way into her dreams. It only made the news worse.

Regardless of what he said, there was no way Bianca could be dead. Gwen had just seen her yesterday at the dinner table. They'd had grilled steaks and Bianca had cooked the potatoes—if Gwen looked, she was sure the knife Bianca had touched was probably still sitting unwashed in the sink. How could it be possible that the woman she'd talked to, and shared a bottle of wine with, was gone this morning? No.

She dabbed her eyes. It wasn't real. A fresh tear twisted down her cheek.

It was stupid, but as she cried, she couldn't handle the thought that Wyatt had seen her turn into a blubbering mess. When he saw her after the last time, she was supposed to be at her best—maybe down a size or two, hair perfectly colored and flung in symmetrical curls over her shoulders like one of those models from the pages of *Country Living*. But no…he had to break her heart—though admittedly, the last time she'd seen him, she may have been the one doing the breaking.

Was that why he had agreed to take on the assignment of telling them about Bianca's death? She wiped the rest of the wetness from her face and stomped down the steps of the porch and into the driveway.

She just needed fresh air—anything to pull her into a different reality, where none of this was really happening.

"Gwen?" Wyatt called after her.

She stopped but she didn't turn around. She couldn't look at him and his ridiculously sexy features. Not right now. Right now she'd like to look at anything but him...the oh-so-confusing him.

"What, Wyatt? What do you want? You gave me the news you came here to give. Now I've got to go to work. This ranch and the cows on it are all we have—if I don't turn a profit this year, it's over." Her knees felt weak, but she refused to let herself to succumb to the feeling. She had to be strong. She had to fake it...at least until he was gone, and then she could turn into a big mess for as long as she needed.

If there was any silver lining to what was happening, it was that her mother had drunk enough whiskey to pass out for at least the rest of the day. The last thing she needed was to have to deal with that train wreck before she had everything figured out—she could only handle one major catastrophe at a time.

"Don't run off, Gwen. I need to ask you a few more questions." He rushed to walk by her side, so she sped up.

"Ask away, but you're going to have to walk because I've got to feed the horses." She motioned toward the red barn that sat in the distance.

"In your nightgown?" he asked, motioning toward the red plaid thing she'd forgotten she was wearing. "And you do know you're wearing slippers, right?"

She stopped and spun to face him, but carefully pulled her nightgown over her moccasins. He was wearing a stupid, charming grin—a grin she wanted to slap right off his face. How dare he, at a time like this?

"What do you want to know?" As she thought about the things he'd want to ask—Bianca's favorite restaurant, where she'd liked to spend her time, her love life—she choked up and had to take a long breath. She couldn't cry again.

He reached up, so slowly that she watched his motion and thought about moving out of the radius of his touch, but she stayed put. He took her shoulder gently and stroked her arm with his thumb. It made her think of her favorite mare, Dancer. The mustang was fifteen, yet anytime she was stressed or acting out, all Gwen had to do to calm her was rub her hands down her flanks and make those same circles with her thumbs.

No matter how much Wyatt might have liked her to be, she wasn't a damned horse that would turn soft under his touch and bend to his wants. He should have known better. It hadn't worked in the two years they had dated in high school either. In fact, it only infuriated her.

She pulled away from his touch. The place his hand had been chilled and she covered it with her own hand, trapping some of the left-over heat.

"Gwen, it's okay to be upset about this. If you want, I can take care of the livestock. Why don't you go inside and lie down? I can come back and talk to you another time if you'd like."

Some of her anger at the world slipped with the kindness in his voice. He wasn't here to hurt her. He was here to do his job. And maybe, just maybe, he was here because he was still her friend and he could look past how she had treated him when they were younger—not that it had been unjustified, her anger toward him, but she should have been kinder. His heart had been just as much on the line as her own.

She ran her hand down her nightgown and started to move back toward the house. Maybe she should lie down, take a break, have a cup of coffee and collect her thoughts. She thought about sending him away, but it made her heart shift in her chest.

"The last thing I want is to be alone right

now." She was surprised by her blunt honesty. It was unlike her, but, then again, nothing about this morning was in the realm of normal. "If you don't have anywhere else to be, maybe you can wait while I get dressed and then take care of the animals. Then we can head up to Bianca's cabin."

Wyatt frowned. "She had a cabin?"

Gwen sighed as she walked back into the house and motioned to her mother's bedroom door as a loud snore escaped from under the door. "We each adopted one of the hands' cabins at the edge of the property. Having a place of your own comes in handy when *she* gets a little too out of hand."

"How often does that kind of thing happen?" His face twisted with concern but not judgment, and it softened some of the hard edges of her feelings toward him.

Most of the time, when people talked to her about her mother's problem, it was with a mixture of pity and judgment. Then again, few people wanted to bring it up. It was like the worst-kept secret of Mystery, Montana, that her mother and her family were one hot mess. In fact, it would probably be only a matter of time before the news of her sister's death would hit the airwaves. She would know as soon as it did because within the hour casseroles would start showing up on their doorstep.

She looked toward her mother's bedroom. At least it was unlikely Carla would get up to answer the door in the condition she was in. Gwen glanced up at the clock. On days like this, when her mother had been drinking all night, Carla normally wouldn't get up until it was time to go to the bar again. Tonight, she'd probably be in hog heaven—getting free drinks from the other lushes and lechers who frequented the bar, all in honor of her daughter's death.

Hate reverberated through her—but the hate wasn't just for her mother, or their situation, or even her sister's death. It was hate for everything.

Her life was such a disaster. And there was nothing she could do about it. No way to control all the emotions that flooded through her. All she could do was feel. She glanced back at Wyatt, staring at him for a moment too long.

"Do you want me to get you something?" he asked, motioning toward her upstairs bedroom. "You can just sit down. I'll grab your gear." His face turned slightly red, as though he'd suddenly realized that "gear" may involve her panties.

She shook her head and walked to the stairs, his embarrassment pulling her back to reality. "I'll be right back."

When she reached her room, it took all her strength not to collapse onto the bed and bury her face into the pillows and scream—yell at the world, tell it of her hate, tell it of her pain, tell it about the injustices that filled her life.

BEING ALONE IN the Johansens' house felt surreal, like somehow he was reliving moments of his past—moments he had fought hard to forget. He walked to the fireplace and looked at the collection of pictures that rested on the mantel. All were covered with a thick layer of dust, forgotten or perhaps intentionally ignored by the women of the house. He rubbed the dust off the closest one. The picture was of a man, whom he recognized as Mr. Johansen, wearing a Hypercolor shirt and drinking a Miller Lite beside a small, white, inflatable kiddie pool. A young blonde girl was splashing water and laughing. The man wasn't smiling, rather he was looking off into the distance as a cigarette trembled on his lip, almost as if he were looking into a future where only tragedy waited.

Carla's snoring sounded from the other room, reminding him of why he'd always hated coming into this house.

He glanced at all the other pictures. None were from any time within the last fifteen years. It was like life had stopped the moment that Mr. Johansen died. He could only imagine what would happen to their lives now that Bianca was gone as well.

Wyatt had to get out. He couldn't let himself get sucked back into this world. Not when it was clear that Gwen could barely tolerate him. He couldn't carry her through this like he used to carry her through the nights her mother had left her alone when Gwen was younger. He couldn't save her—he'd already tried.

He rushed outside to the barn. Horses he could understand. Women, on the other hand... Women were an entirely different issue.

One of the barn cats sauntered over to him as he made his way inside. It wrapped itself around his legs, rubbing against him. He picked it up and scratched under its chin as it purred and kneaded the front of his shirt. As he stood there stroking the long gray hair of the cat, he glanced up at the hayloft. They had spent so many hours up there, just him and Gwen. They had been able to talk for hours; it had always seemed like they would never run out of things to discuss. They'd had this wonderful bond with each other that, no matter how many women he'd dated since, he was never able to re-create. Maybe it was the one thing he missed most about her—their deep bond, so strong that he could feel it even when no words were spoken.

Putting the cat down, he moved over to the bales of hay. He pulled off flakes and dropped them into the stalls for each of the horses. Though it was cold, in an effort to keep the hay from digging into his uniform, he stripped off his uniform shirt and his ballistics vest, leaving only his tank top. It felt good, the chill of the winter air, the scratching of the hay against his arms and the smell of horses on his skin.

He wasn't involved with the business of his family's ranch enough anymore to really help in the everyday comings and goings, and sometimes, when he caught a whiff of fresh hay or the heady fragrance of sweet oats, he missed being more available.

There was a thin cough, and he turned around. Gwen stood in the barn's doorway, looking at him in a way that made him wonder if it was attraction or revulsion. He moved to grab his shirt and vest, but she stopped him with a wave of the hand.

"It's fine. Just be comfortable. There's not going to be anyone up at the cabin who's going to care if you're wearing your uniform. At least not since…" She trailed off, as though she couldn't bring herself to talk about Bianca.

He grabbed his shirt and slipped it over his tank top anyway. It felt strange to be standing in front of her even semi undressed. In all their time together, they hadn't taken things to a deeply physical level.

He stared at her for a moment, wondering if she was still the same girl he had known before, or if she had given up on her quest to wait until marriage. He'd always appreciated, or at least respected, the effort it took to restrict oneself from pleasures of the flesh, but it wasn't a dogma that he had been able to follow.

She looked disappointed when he put on the shirt—or was she relieved? It would have been so much easier if he could just read minds.

The drive to the cabin was short, but the entire time he had been glancing over at her, wondering what she was thinking and trying to hold back from asking her the million questions running through his mind. Most were stupid, insipid... Whether or not she liked her job at the ranch, what it was like to still be living with her mother or, for that matter, why she was still choosing to live with Carla. No matter if Gwen stayed or went, her mother would continue her self-destructive behavior. It was only a matter of time...

He pulled to a stop in front of the cabin that Gwen had directed them to. There was a small chicken coop outside it, and there was a bevy of hens clucking inside, waiting to be fed.

Gwen nearly jumped out of the patrol unit and ran to the chickens. She grabbed the bucket out of the galvanized can beside the coop and poured the cracked corn into the trough. The hens came running in a flurry of feathers and clucks.

He stood and watched her, taking in the sight of her body flexing as she moved around the coop. She seemed nervous, but he could have her all wrong. Most people he could read at a glance. The ability to tell whether someone was lying, hiding something or telling the truth came with the job. Yet he didn't have the same innate gift when it came to Gwen. She was his enigma.

"I'm going to go inside. Feel free to take your time out here, okay?" he asked.

"Yeah. That's fine. I'll be out here if you need me." She didn't bother to look back at him, fully consumed with opening the hen-house to collect this morning's eggs. This late in the year, without a light in the henhouse, they both knew that there wouldn't be many, if any, eggs, but he didn't say anything.

He walked to the front of the cabin. Its walls were made of the aged, gray logs like those from the pioneering days when the town had been founded. The wooden door sat crooked in the frame, listing like Bianca's drunk mother. For a moment, he wondered if Bianca had left it like that on purpose as a re-minder of what she had to move past in order to live her own life.

He pushed the door open. His breath caught in his throat. Papers were strewn around the room, every drawer was open and the couch cushions had been thrown from their places, one precariously close to the woodstove. Ei-ther Bianca was the kind who never cleaned, or someone had turned the place over.

In an effort to avoid causing Gwen any more emotional trauma, he walked inside and closed the door. He pulled out his camera and clicked a few pictures. It was odd how, in just a few short hours, his assignment had led him from thinking this was a natural death to a possible suicide to now something much more sinister.

He couldn't say if Bianca's death was a murder. Nothing about Bianca's body or presentation at the scene had pointed toward a struggle or malevolent act, but his instincts told him to push the investigation deeper.

Unfortunately, he was leaving in a few days for a prisoner transfer in Alaska. If he followed his instincts, he could be wrapped up in this investigation for weeks—and he had been wrong before. Just a year ago, he'd wasted time investigating a case similar to this. Maybe it had been his bravado, or his need to follow every lead, but he'd spent two weeks tracking down every thread just to find out from the medical examiner that their victim had died of a methadone overdose. The guy had been seeking euphoria—and all he'd found was the grave.

Wyatt walked through the cabin, careful not to disturb things in case he needed to call in his team of investigators—and what a team it was, two of the least-trained CSI guys anyone had ever met. In fact, he wasn't sure if Lyle and Steve had ever gone to college, or if their certification had come from some online university where they never had to actually set foot on a crime scene to graduate.

There was a squeak from behind him. Gwen stood there, her hands over her mouth as she stared at the mess of papers, clothes and overturned chairs.

"Do you know who would have done this?" he asked, staring at her.

Her eyes were wide and she dropped her balled fists to her sides. She glanced at him and shook her head.

He'd been wrong about Gwen. He'd thought he couldn't read her. Yet when she looked at him, he could see she was lying.

Chapter Three

They'd gone through everything. Or at least it felt like it. Gwen closed her sister's dresser drawer with a thump.

"Anything?" Wyatt asked, motioning toward the drawer that had been filled with her sister's bras.

From an objective point of view, it struck her as a bit funny and maybe a touch endearing that Wyatt, the type-A man who seemed most at home in his squad car, was squeamish about riffling through her sister's underwear drawer. In high school he had seen just about every pair of panties that Gwen had owned, though things had always stopped there.

She glanced over at him. He had been good-looking back in the day, but he was nothing then compared to the man he had become—the man she had just watched throwing bales of hay around like they were pillows rather than seventy-five pounds of dead weight. If things had been different, if she could have ignored the pull of reality, she could have stood there all day and watched him sweat.

He brushed past her, leaving the room, and he still carried the sweet scent of hay, horses and leather. The heady aroma made her lift her head as she drew in a long whiff of the man she had once loved.

It wasn't that she hadn't been in relationships, it had only been a few months—wait, a year—since her last thing. It hadn't quite been a Facebook-official relationship. No, it had been more of a burger-and-a-beer/Netflix-and-chill kind of thing. No real feelings beyond lust and the occasional need for a back rub. It had been great until he had suddenly disappeared, and two months later she had seen the guy's engagement to another woman splashed across their tiny paper, the *Mystery Daily*.

The news hadn't hurt so much as caused her the emotional whiplash that came with being so quickly replaced. A month after the engagement announcement, she still hadn't gotten an invite to the wedding that nearly the entire population of the small town had received. She had always resigned herself to the belief that everyone knew everyone's business in Mystery—yet a few had still asked her why she hadn't gone and she had been forced to tactfully remove herself from the conversation.

"You okay?" Wyatt surprised her as he touched her shoulder ever so lightly.

How long had he been standing there?

She nodded, thankful he'd pulled her from her thoughts. "What do you think they were looking for in here?" She motioned around her sister's cabin.

"First, we don't know if this was a *they* kind of situation. Maybe your sister did this. There's no proof that her death was anything unnatural, or more than a—"

Suicide.

He didn't need to finish the sentence to inflict the pain that came with the word.

"My sister wouldn't kill herself. You knew her. You saw her almost every week. Do you really think that she could do something like that—or like this?" She waved at the strewn couch cushions. "No one turns over their own place."

He looked away, but she could see in the

way his eyes darkened that he was already thinking the same thing.

The desk where her sister's laptop normally sat was conspicuously empty. But the printer was still there, and there was a wastebasket on the ground, its contents strewn across the floor like everything else in the cabin. She pulled away from Wyatt's touch and picked up one of the balled-up pieces of paper. Uncurling the wad, she found an email. It was dated November 27—one week earlier. She didn't recognize the email address or the long bits of code that her sister included in the printout. It looked like it had been pulled from the printer before it was done, and long dabs of ink were smudged down the paper's length.

"What's that?" Wyatt asked, sidestepping her as though he was trying his best not to touch her again.

"I dunno… It looks odd, though," she said, flipping the page so he could see.

It was probably nothing. She crumpled the paper in her hands and, picking up the garbage can, dropped it in. Maybe she was looking too hard and trying to see things that were not really there—she glanced at Wyatt—especially when it came to him.

He bent down and picked up another of the

papers. He sucked in a breath as he looked over the page.

"What is it?"

He held the paper and didn't move, almost as though if he stood still she wouldn't have asked the question.

She stepped closer and looked over his shoulder.

The email was almost identical to the one she had picked up, but instead of black smudges of ink, the message was there in its entirety:

RUN AND LIVE.
STAY AND DIE.
CHOICE IS YOURS.

Why hadn't Bianca told anyone about the threat? And why, oh, why, had she chosen to stay?

HE SENT A picture of the email to the head of the IT department, Max, along with a promise that if Max got back to Wyatt within a day, Wyatt would personally take him on a ride-along. He hated ride-alongs, especially when it entailed taking a person who would ask more questions than a kid on Mountain

Dew. Yet without a doubt, it would expedite the process—and he needed answers as soon as possible.

He was having one heck of a time focusing on anything other than the way he wanted to take Gwen into his arms and hold her. She looked so broken. Every time she stopped moving, she zoned out, almost as though she couldn't find the strength to start moving again.

He knew the feeling all too well. It was why he never stopped—the moment you started bringing up the pain was the moment the world collapsed around you. In his line of work, it was best to just bury the past...along with anything else that kept him up at night. Bianca's death was definitely going to fall in that category.

Bianca had looked nearly pristine when he'd arrived on scene. Her hair was pulled back into her signature ponytail and her scrubs were still clean, like she'd just pulled them out of the dryer before she had come out to the ranch.

His heart sank at the thought of the ranch. No wonder Gwen was so lost. She had so many reasons to be angry. So many people she could point a finger at, and no one more

than him. Even in the event of Bianca's death
he could be held responsible—at least tangen-
tially. He had likely been home, resting com-
fortably after a long day on shift. If he'd been
more involved in the comings and goings of
Dunrovin, if he had agreed to feed the horses,
or been around at all, maybe she would still
be alive. Not that Gwen knew that—but her
being unaware didn't relieve any of his guilt.

Gwen was doing it again, staring at the
floor like it was the exact spot where Bianca
had been found. His hands twitched with the
need to feel her in them.

"Let's go. I'll run you back home."

She jerked as though she had forgotten
where they were.

He took care to lock the door to the cabin
to stop anyone from coming back in, and then
he held her hand on the way back to the car.
Her fingers were limp in his. She was a ghost
of what she used to be—strong and hot, as
wild and free as the Montana mountains and
wilderness that surrounded them. He wished
he could pull her from her stupor, pull her
back to the land of the living instead of falling deeper into the pit of the despondent.

It wasn't long before they were bumping
down the Widow Maker Ranch's long, snowy

driveway, laden with potholes and ruts left over from hard use in summer and fall. As Wyatt twisted and turned, trying to avoid the worst of the bumps and the largest snowdrifts, he was reminded of how life was just like a road—full of obstacles and dangers.

Something hit the car and he tapped on the brakes as he tried to identify the source of the sound. There was another thump and he pulled to a stop.

"What was that?" Gwen asked, looking around.

Pastures lined both sides of the drive, grasses so tall that even in the snow it looked like they were in a sea of brown reeds—making it nearly impossible to see who or what could have been responsible for the sound.

"Stay inside," he said as he stepped out of the car.

He walked to the front of the patrol unit. On its fender were the scattered, oozing remnants of two eggs. He turned just in time to see Carla holding a carton and pulling her arm back to take aim.

"Stop, Carla!" he ordered, his voice hard-edged and full of authority.

The egg flew through the air, missing him

by just a few inches and smacking against the car's windshield.

Gwen stepped out of the car and slammed the door. "Mother, what in the hell do you think you're doing?"

Her mother smeared her forearm under her nose and dropped the carton of eggs, its contents rolling on the ground at her feet. "He's a bastard…" She motioned to Wyatt as though he couldn't hear her. "It's his damned fault." She reached behind her back.

His fine-tuned senses kicked into full gear. "Hands where I can see them!" he yelled.

Carla laughed, her sound high and malicious. "You don't get to order me around. I've known you since you were born. You loved my daughter. You knew Jimmy. Yet you did nothing…nothing to protect my Bianca. You let your family's demons take her."

There were any number of demons she could have been talking about when it came to his family, but in this moment it didn't matter—all that mattered was what she was holding behind her back and what she planned on doing with it.

"Put your hands where I can see them." He slowly reached down for the Taser on his utility belt.

The last thing he wanted to do was to tase Gwen's mother. Things were already tense enough, but no matter what his feelings toward Gwen and her family were, his job and their safety came first.

"I don't want to hurt you...I don't..." Carla said as she moved toward him, her motions jerky as though her body and her mind were in disagreement. "But you and your family... You all keep ruining my life. You want to take everything from me."

"We didn't take anything from you." He knew he shouldn't argue with the grief-crazed woman, but he couldn't hear her drag his family through the mud anymore. She needed to be pulled back to reality.

She dropped her hand to her side. In her grip was a snub-nosed revolver.

Either she was going to shoot him or herself—either way, he couldn't allow her to keep that gun in her possession.

"Drop the gun, Carla," he said.

She looked at him, and a tear slipped down her cheek. As the wind kicked up, he could smell the strong scent of whiskey wafting from her—even stronger than before.

She shook her head, the action slow and deliberate.

"Mother. No. Don't do this," Gwen said. "You can't play at this. Not again. Wyatt is a deputy. He has every right to shoot you if you lift that gun. Drop. It. Now."

Not again? Was Carla's threat something she did on a regular basis?

He thought his family had the corner on putting the *fun* in dysfunctional.

Gwen stepped around the car and moved toward her mother.

"No," he ordered, putting his arm out and trying to stop her without actually losing sight of the gun. "Stay back, Gwen." He tried to hedge his tone between the hard edge of work and the softness of the feelings he still carried for her, but it came out much sharper than he intended.

Gwen looked at him like he had struck her.

He chastised himself, he'd screwed that all up, but now wasn't the time to fully explain himself. "I don't want her to hurt you."

"She's my mother," she spat out. "She's not dangerous. Really. You need to trust me."

He felt the slice of her words as she cut away at his flaw—trust had never been his strong suit and she knew it. Why did she have to call him out at a time like this?

If something happened, if Carla pulled that

trigger, he would have to answer to those above him. They would never understand if he went against procedure—even for a woman he used to know and her daughter, whom he wanted to get to know again.

"Your mother or not, Gwen, she can't do this." He raised his Taser. "This is the last time I ask, Carla," he said, moving into range. "If you don't put the gun down, I will be forced to tase you. Your choice."

Carla lifted the gun.

"Wyatt, no!" Gwen yelled.

He pulled the trigger.

Carla hit the ground, convulsing as the electricity pulsed through her.

He ran to her side and kicked the gun from her hand before picking it up and opening the cylinder to look for rounds. The gun was empty.

Chapter Four

The next morning, Wyatt puttered around his trailer on the edge of the Dunrovin Ranch. Sleep had been elusive, and as he waited for the coffee to fill his cup, his mind wandered to Gwen and Carla. He shouldn't have taken Carla down. Then again, what choice had she given him? He'd warned her—repeatedly. Did she think he was bluffing? That he wouldn't pull the trigger?

If he was good at anything it was falling back onto his training—and he was a better officer for it, though it didn't always make him a better person. There was a certain safety and comfort that came with being inflexible.

He couldn't be like Gwen—she seemed to have her emotions and well-being dictated by the people in her life all the time. For as long as he had known her, she had been living her life in accordance with her mother's ever-changing needs. In a way, he pitied her for her role as caregiver. No wonder she hadn't wanted to be in a major relationship when they were younger—her life was already overtaken by the emotional needs of her mother. Were things any different now, or was she still emotionally unavailable?

He grabbed his coffee, slipped on his utility belt and moved toward the front door. Work waited. He needed to figure out exactly what happened to Bianca before things could get any more confusing with Gwen.

His phone pinged with an email. It was IT. He sipped the hot black coffee as he opened the message.

Fitz—
Took a look at the printout of the email you sent me. Looks like it was originally sent from a computer at the Mystery County Public Library from a one-use email account. Hope that helps. Let me know if you got any more questions.

Can't wait for the ride-along. Next week?
—Max

That was one ride-along that wouldn't really be worth it. Max was a great guy, but the information he'd sent was nearly useless. The only thing Wyatt could pull from it was that whoever had made the threat was probably a local.

The library was completely outdated; its desktop computers were still the same ones used during the advent of dial-up. No one went there to use the computers. The beasts were so slow that most people avoided them. Maybe he could run with that—the librarians might remember someone who had used them to send Bianca the threatening email. If everything went smoothly, he could get to the bottom of the email by the end of the day, Gwen could once again move to the back of his mind and things could return to his habitual, inflexible normal.

He opened the door.

Leaning against the fence was Gwen. Her long blond hair was pulled back into a ponytail as high and tight as her expression. She was looking out into the field, watching as two of his mother's mares nibbled at the bits of grass sticking out of the snow.

"How long have you been out here?"

She turned slightly to face him, but she

didn't greet him with a smile. "Long enough to know that you slept in."

He glanced down at his phone. It was 8:00 a.m. Most ranchers were up at five in order to get the daily chores taken care of. When he'd been working on the ranch in high school he'd followed that schedule, but now that he was on his own, he rarely forced himself to get out of bed that early. Yet Gwen undoubtedly still thought he was the kid he had once been—what would he have to do to prove that he'd changed?

"Long night," he said, but the moment he said it, he wished he hadn't brought it up. The last thing he wanted to do was talk about why and who had kept him awake—or the guilt he felt about his action with Carla. Nothing good would come of bringing up the events of yesterday.

Gwen lifted her chin, but thankfully didn't say anything.

Maybe she didn't want to talk about it either.

He was tempted to apologize, but he couldn't say he was sorry for doing what had to be done, and he didn't want to start a fight, so he just kept his mouth shut. He clicked the door shut behind him and made his way out to her. He leaned against the fence beside her.

She smelled like a fresh shower and the sweet fragrance of roses. It was the same shampoo she had been using since they were young, and the smell made him remember the nights they had spent making out in the bed of his truck. He'd loved those nights under the stars, flirting with the boundaries of their relationship. His fingers twitched as he recalled running them up the soft skin of her belly, his touch only to be trailed with his languishing, hungry kiss. He'd wanted to make love to her so badly.

He moved, readjusting his body, which was responding to his memories. That was all they were—memories. They were as the seasons, the heat of summer all too soon replaced by the chill of the fall.

She stepped away from him, reached down and scooped a bit of the snow together, balling it. She laughed as she pitched it at him. Most of it disintegrated in the air before a tiny bit splattered on his jacket.

"Hey, now, what was that?" he asked with a laugh. He reached down and made a snowball and gently lofted it toward her.

She ducked with a laugh and it breezed

past her. "Missed me," she teased, sticking her tongue out at him.

It reminded him of when they were younger, full of life and joy. It was as if they were innocent again, and it made him long for what they had once been.

She wiped the bits of snow off her hands. "I stopped by hoping you would show me where you found Bianca." Her voice was tinged with sadness, and it made him wish she would just go back to throwing snowballs.

He glanced in the direction of the main house that, from where they were standing, was completely out of view thanks to a large stand of cottonwoods. The barns were behind the house, but he could have drawn them in complete detail from memory, down to the tiny carving in the hayloft of *W+G 4Ever* he'd cut into the soft wood when they were kids.

"There's nothing there. It wasn't much of a crime scene."

"You didn't think it was a murder either, remember?"

Ouch. He thought about arguing with her about what exactly he was and wasn't allowed to do with his investigations, and what he'd been presented with on scene, but he bit his tongue. Apparently she was still in the anger stage of her grief. Next came depression, at least for most people, but knowing Gwen as well as he did, he doubted that she would let him see her like that again.

He rubbed his fingers together as he recalled brushing her tears from her cheeks when she'd collapsed on the floor. It probably wasn't normal for him to feel this way, but he appreciated that moment of weakness when he'd told her about Bianca's death. For once, he'd gotten a real reaction—a response not muted by her strength or her desire to veil the truth. Getting to have the real her was another thing he missed about their dating.

It was a rare thing in this world to know the essence of a person—especially in a small town where everyone feared the jaw-jacking of the neighbors. Any little thing could be a full-blown phone-tree emergency. It was like living in a game of telephone. What may have started out as something innocent enough would be a prison-worthy offense in under twenty-four hours—and that fear kept everything muted, even emotions.

It was maybe the thing he hated the most about living in a small town.

He pushed off the fence and walked toward his patrol unit. Gwen had parked her father's old beat-up Ford in front of his one-car garage.

She followed close behind him. "Are you going to take me over there? Or do I just need to go and figure it out?"

Yep, definitely still in the anger phase.

"In the car," he said, answering her with the same level of shortness.

It wasn't really a distance worth driving, but he immersed himself in the silence between them—letting it remind him of exactly all the reasons he should cap any of his nostalgic feelings for the girl he'd once known. The Gwen beside him, while she had many of the old habits he had once loved her for, was not the same.

He would give almost anything to see that smile he'd fallen in love with, the one he'd caught a glimpse of when she pitched the snowball at him. He'd always remember that girl.

He parked in front of the stables. A little girl was standing by the front door; her hands were red from the cold but she still had her thumb planted in her mouth. He smiled as he got out of the car and gave an acknowledging nod to his former sister-in-law Alli Fitzgerald's daughter. He'd never really cared for Alli—especially after she had cheated on Waylon—but he'd always had a soft spot for her daughter and was glad that she had chosen to raise her child on the ranch.

The little munchkin, Winnie, had curly brown hair and a smile complete with all of her baby teeth in their gapped and crooked glory. And when she smiled at him, everyone on the entire ranch knew that he was mush. Whatever the girl wanted…it was hers.

He walked around to open the door for Gwen.

"How's it goin', Win?" he asked, sending the little girl a playful grin.

The two-year-old bounded over to him, throwing her arms around his knees. "Wy-ant!" she cried, saying his name with two distinct syllables. "You bring candy?"

He reached into the breast pocket of his uniform where he always carried fun-sized banana taffies for Winnie. "Oh, no," he teased. "I'm all out!"

Her plump cheeks fell and her smile disappeared as she looked up at him. "Wy-ant… Don't tease da poor girl," she said it with all seriousness, but he couldn't help but laugh as her high-pitched voice mimicked her mother's words.

"Oh, well, if you say so." He pulled the candy from his pocket and handed it to Winnie, who took it and ran toward the barn and out of the vicinity of anywhere her mother might see her gobble the treat.

Winnie turned back as she moved to slip through the barn door. "Thank you, Wy-ant."

Gwen stood next to him. "Looks like you have a fan."

He looked at her and smiled. "She is something special," he said, wanting to add that the girl wasn't the only special one in his life, but he stopped.

Gwen looked at him and moved to speak, but stopped and then walked to the barn where Winnie had disappeared. "Where did it happen?"

He motioned forward, opened the door for her and followed her inside. The lights were on, illuminating the darkened stalls. It was quiet since the horses had already been fed and turned out for the day. The place smelled like hay and horses, a smell that always reminded him of home.

"We found her in the back pen, just there," he said, motioning to the stall.

Gwen stood still, staring in the direction he had pointed. Aside from it being the place where they'd found Bianca's body, it was like every other barn—stacks of hay, the tack room, stalls and a door leading to the pasture. Yet Gwen was holding her arm around her body like this was the first time they'd ever been inside, even though there was evidence in the hayloft to the contrary.

Her gaze moved to the ladder that led up to the hayloft, and for a moment, he swore he saw a smile flicker over her lips. Was she thinking about the last time they had stepped up those rungs as well?

He walked around her, hoping she was envisioning all the possibilities of giving him one more shot in the hayloft. Moving to the stall, he looked to the spot where they had found Bianca. For a moment, he could see her there again. At the time, there had been talk about calling her family in, but he was glad now, looking back, that they hadn't. Some things couldn't be unseen. It would be hard enough for Gwen to see Bianca in the casket—the last thing she needed was to see her sister sitting in the middle of the horse stall surrounded by dirty hay, water buckets and the hooves of a hurt and scared mare.

The horse was gone and the stall had been recently cleaned so well that he could smell the strong, suspicious scent of bleach. That was unlike his mother or the staff—normally they never used bleach out here. Some things weren't going to get completely clean no matter how much scrubbing they did, and a horse stall was one of them.

"What happened to the horse—is she okay?" Gwen asked.

The wood of the door was rounded and smoothed by the years of horses chewing it, but as he took his hand away it still scraped at his skin.

"My mother had another vet come in and take a look at her. Luckily, the horse's leg wasn't broken, just a sprain."

"I'm glad the horse is going to be okay." She said it like it carried some measure of comfort that only one of the beings in this stall had lost its life. "Bianca would have liked to have known the horse was okay, I'm sure."

"I'm sure she's watching down." As he spoke, he knew it was a platitude.

Gwen glanced over at him and put her hand on top of his. "Thanks. I know you don't mean it, but thanks."

Seriously, it was like she could read his mind sometimes and it scared the bejeezus out of him. As it was, however, with her warm hand on his, he would take whatever he could get. It was better than having her angry.

He took her hand in his. "I do mean it. Sort of."

"You don't believe in that stuff, remember?"

He shrugged. "What I believe doesn't matter. What matters is that your sister was a good person. If there is any justice in this world, her soul will rest in peace, maybe where she can watch down on you and help keep you from finding yourself in too much trouble." He smiled, trying to lighten the mood. He hated talk of death.

"If there was any justice in this world, Wyatt, she wouldn't have been killed. And I wouldn't be standing in the middle of the crime scene."

"Actually," a woman said, her voice cutting through the tension, "you aren't really standing in the middle of the crime scene. Bianca died inside the stall."

He turned to see Alli standing there, Winnie in hand, staring at them. Gwen pulled her fingers from his, and as much as he loved Winnie, he silently wished they hadn't been interrupted.

"Heya, Alli. You're right, but this is still

part of the scene," he said. "Come here, Winnie-girl."

Winnie let go of her mother's hand and scampered over, and he picked her up. She was heavy in his arms in a way that made him wish, for half a second, that he had a child of his own.

Gwen looked over at him and smiled, but the action was short-lived.

"You know, Wyatt, you don't have to give Winnie a treat every time you see her," Alli grumbled. "She's getting spoiled. Soon she's going to be a brat if you keep it up."

He lifted Winnie so he could look up into her face. He turned her from right to left as though he was inspecting her. "Yep. Nope. Don't see a brat here. Just see a few bats in the cave."

Winnie giggled, the sound was infectious and he caught himself laughing with her.

"What, don't you ever pick those boogies?" he teased.

Winnie reached up and stuck her finger in her nose. She lifted her finger for him to see. "Look, I get them boogies!" she answered excitedly.

"You're just like your brother," Alli said, her tone heavy with dislike. She reached over and grabbed Winnie and set her back on the ground. "Go wash your hands, girl."

Winnie gave him a backward wave as she escaped the confines of the barn and the castigation of her mother.

"The gardens looked good this year," he said, trying to make small talk with Alli.

She shrugged. "I'll do better next year. It was just too dry a summer."

He'd tried to work in the gardens one year, as his family sold their vegetables and fruits at the local farmer's market every Saturday in the warm months, but he'd found in a single month that he had a brown thumb rather than a green one. Though, admittedly, he had been working there with their old gardener, Bernard, who'd had even less of an amicable nature than Alli. Not all professional gardeners he'd met were light on personality, but it seemed like the last couple his mother had employed were no Bob Hopes.

Then again, his mother hadn't really hired Alli so much as been forced to bring her into the fold when Waylon had eloped with her. Now Wyatt's brother had been gone for almost three years, but here they were stuck with the only part of him that he'd left behind.

Alli hadn't always been rough to be around,

but the day Waylon left everything likable about Alli had gone with him.

"How were the tomatoes this year?" Gwen asked, in what he assumed was some kind of olive branch.

"Not as good as I woulda liked, but I did pretty good at the market. The people in Kalispell ate them up. Get it?" She laughed at her own pun.

Gwen gave a light, polite laugh.

"That's great." He tried not to sound too dismissive, but with everything going on he wanted to get moving instead of getting stuck making small talk with the woman who betrayed his brother. "Do you know who cleaned up the stall? I'd like to talk to them." He dipped his chin in the direction of the bleach jug that sat in the corner near the front door.

She looked in the direction and frowned. "I dunno. People have been coming and going ever since your crew came through and took the body out." She turned to Gwen. "I'm sorry for your loss. It's always hard losing someone you love."

Gwen nodded in acknowledgment. "By chance, did anyone see a bag around here?" She stuck out her hands in measurement. "It was black, about yea big?"

"I didn't see nothing. I ain't been around here too much. Just saw your car out front and Winnie was munching on the candy. Put two and two together and thought I'd come say hi." She shrugged. "If you're looking for something specific, you might want to ask your mom, Wyatt. She's been poking around in here."

It didn't surprise him that his mom would have been spending her time in here after everything had gone down—of all the folks at Dunrovin, she'd taken Bianca's death the hardest. She had a soft spot for the vet.

"I'll chat with her," he said, all too aware that in the next conversation he had with his family he would have to tell them what direction the investigation had headed.

The news wouldn't come without blowback. And that was to say nothing about what the death would do to the tourism that kept the ranch afloat. If anyone caught wind that this was a possible murder case, it would undoubtedly hurt his parents' bottom line.

"Do you know where they dumped the hay from the stall?" Gwen asked, pulling him from thoughts of his family.

"Oh, yeah," Alli said, her sullen frown returning. "They always take that out to the gardens. It's high in nitrogen so I'm always making it into compost for the beds. Why?"

Gwen gave him a look, a look that told him that no matter how crappy he thought some of his investigations had been, they were going to be heading to entirely new levels.

"No, Gwen." He shook his head. "The team already went through the stall before. They didn't find anything. There's no point going through...anything."

"If you don't want to get your hands dirty, Wyatt, that's fine," she said, but her tone told him there would be worse things than horse manure to deal with if he didn't play along. "But this wasn't their sister. I need to do everything in my power to figure out what exactly happened to Bianca. You loved her once too. I know. We both owe her to try our damnedest to solve her murder."

Alli visibly twitched. "Murder?"

No. He hadn't been ready for the rest of the world to learn what they had started to uncover.

He shook his head violently...almost too hard to be convincing. "No, not murder. Bianca wasn't murdered."

Alli raised an eyebrow. "Then what happened to her?"

He took Gwen by the hand and led her toward the back door of the barn and the gardens. "I don't know yet, Alli…but that's what we're hoping to find out." Even if it meant getting his hands dirty.

They grabbed a couple of pitchforks from the wall of tools and made their way from the barn.

"Good luck," Alli called from behind them.

He couldn't blame her for not joining them. Right now, he wished he was anywhere— even the prisoner transfer in Alaska—rather than here and having to do what needed to be done.

As they approached the mound of compost, Gwen pulled a bandanna out of her pocket and tied it over her face in what Wyatt assumed was an effort to save herself from breathing in the scent of manure for the next hour.

"Are you sure that you really want to do this?" he asked, sticking in his pitchfork and flipping through a frozen pile of the detritus. He could think of a thousand things he would rather being doing than going through a pile of compost for evidence they weren't going to find.

She gave him a glance and her face was pinched tight, as though she was as disgusted by this as he was. "Just look." She scraped at the pile.

He followed her lead, but all he could think of was how close they were and how much he'd rather be anywhere else with her.

He worked his way through the hay as diligently as he could, given the circumstances. After ten minutes, the cold had started to nibble at his fingertips. They were never going to find anything.

"Look…" she said, leaning down and pointing at something from her side of the mound.

He moved closer to see what she was looking at. There, lying in the heap of refuse, was what looked like a small white pen. Bits of frozen hay were stuck to its sides.

"What is it?" he asked, moving so he could take a closer look.

"It's a used needle," she said. "And I bet you we just found the thing that killed my sister. Now we just need to find out who was holding it—her, or someone who wanted her dead."

Chapter Five

Wyatt took the syringe and headed to Kali-spell to hand deliver it to the crime lab. In truth, the last thing Gwen had expected was to find anything in the compost pile—it had been done on a whim, a dare she thought he wouldn't accept. He had surprised her with his willingness to go along with her.

Was it possible he was trying to impress her, or was he just trying to do whatever was necessary to keep her happy and quiet?

She glanced down at her phone and pulled up his picture from when they were kids. He still had the same wide jaw and caramel-col-ored eyes of the boy she had once loved, but now there was something different—some-thing that seemed to haunt him.

Then again, she was the one with the most ghosts.

She flipped to the next picture, the one of Bianca holding a handful of purple and yellow wildflowers. In the photo, Bianca was laughing, her mouth open with glee and her eyes full of life. She looked beautiful. It was one of those perfect moments when everything was going her way, and all the best of life was coming together.

How quickly those moments faded and reality closed in, and the ghosts that floated through their lives returned. Gwen had her own secrets, but none were quite like Bianca's. Gwen's sister had a penchant for living life with one foot in the world of danger.

Gwen slipped her phone back in her pocket as she thought about what she had to do. Her gut ached. Some of the secrets between her and her sister weren't things she wanted to explore. Yet she needed to talk to her sister's darkest secret, William Poe—no matter how badly she hated the man and the role he'd forced her sister to play.

She glanced at her watch. The roads were a bit icy, but if she hurried she could catch him before he went to work and avoid Wyatt finding out what she feared telling him. Wyatt had always been kind to her sister and given her the benefit of the doubt about her choices, but if he found out what she'd really been doing, all of his good opinions of her would probably fly out the window. And if he wasn't on her and Bianca's side, it was unlikely that he'd put everything behind this investigation. He needed to be emotionally connected and remember Bianca as the person she really was—instead of the warped version that William had required her to become.

If Gwen was going to protect her sister's honor, she couldn't let anyone else—not even Wyatt—find out the truth.

She started the old Ford, letting it smoke and sputter to life. It rumbled as though even the truck questioned her plan, but instead of listening she pushed it in gear and drove toward the one place she said she was never going to return to.

As she made her way down the frontage road that led to William's house, she thought of the last time she'd seen the man. He and Bianca had gotten into a fight, and Bianca had called her—it was how Gwen had found out about their illicit affair. When Gwen had arrived at the man's house, William had been standing on his porch half naked, screaming at Bianca and calling her every foul name Gwen could have imagined. Bianca had scurried from the house, wrapped in nothing more than his hundred-dollar sheet. Tears had been streaming down Bianca's face as she threw herself onto the truck's bench seat.

Gwen glanced over at the truck's seat. It had been just over six months ago, and though she had told Bianca to kick the man to the curb, as far as she knew, Bianca had gone back to him whenever his wife was out of town.

Hopefully William's wife wasn't out of town now. There would be nothing better than confronting William about his mistress, and what he knew about her death, in front of his wife. In so many ways, Bianca's life reminded Gwen of one of the many soap operas they had grown up watching in the days when they had only three channels—and the only thing on television when they got home from school was *Days of Our Lives*.

She smiled at the thought of them balled up on the couch watching as the show revealed the latest secret baby. It was one of the reasons she had been hooked on reading romance novels. Even now her bedside table was covered with this month's latest releases. It was her favorite vice.

It wasn't far from Dunrovin to the Poes',

but then again, nothing in this town was really that far. In fact, with a pair of binoculars and a high vantage, she was almost certain that she could see most of the town and its goings-on. The lack of privacy made the hair on the back of her neck stand up. She hated the thought of how easy it was for her life to be tracked—who knew who all was watching.

The Poes' garage was separate from the house. A long, covered walkway was the only thing connecting them. As Gwen drove up the driveway, she noticed William standing in the walkway like he was waiting for her. He looked out of place standing there surrounded by the pine garlands with pretty white lights and the Santa Claus decoration in his front yard—it was almost like he was normal.

It gave her chills. He wasn't giving her a look that was particularly dangerous. It seemed more as though her presence, while not a surprise, was a nuisance. Had he had some clue she would be on her way to see him? Maybe he heard about Bianca's death and was just waiting for her to arrive. Either way, the dislike she felt for him intensified.

He ran his fingers through his waxed hair, making sure everything was in place, and readjusted his suit jacket before hurrying toward her truck. He motioned for her to stay put. She rushed to turn off the truck and slip out its door. She wanted to make him as uncomfortable as possible. He deserved to feel pressured by her being there.

"Gwen, why are you here?" It sounded more like an accusation than a question.

"You don't know?" She tried to read his reaction, but as a semi-politician his face remained placid. It made her hatred toward the county tax appraiser tick upward.

"Gwen, I don't have time for you or your sister's games. She needs to just accept that we are over. I'm tired of her trying to manipulate me and you can tell her I said that."

So they weren't together. Or was he just playing some kind of game with her?

"You should tell her that yourself." She felt the weight of the unspoken truth on her tongue, but she wasn't ready to tell him about Bianca's death. He didn't deserve anything… no measure of kindness or pity.

He turned to walk away, but she grabbed his arm and forced him to turn and face her again.

"Gwen, I have to get to work. Seriously, just tell Bianca this has to stop. I'm not taking her back."

She hated the fact that she had no idea what William was talking about. Clearly he and Bianca had broken up, but when and why? Not for the first time, she wished she had talked to her sister more. Yet neither of them had really wanted to bring up the issue of William because Gwen hated the man, and she assumed Bianca was ashamed of her decision to be with such a shady person.

William glanced toward his house, where the kitchen window looked out toward the driveway.

"Is your wife inside?" she asked, taking some small measure of comfort that Monica might bear witness to some of her husband's secrets.

His eyes widened with what she assumed was fear. For a moment, she considered going in there and telling Monica exactly what kind of man William was. The poor woman needed to know the things he did when she was out of sight. Then again, some secrets didn't need to see the light of day—especially when it involved her sister's memory.

Regardless of her desire to reveal the truth, he needed to fear her and what chaos she could bring to his life. She felt a bit ruthless, but she didn't care. The man was one of the reasons she feared dating again. If all men were like him, with questionable morals and sharp, cutting tongues, she could live without them.

Wyatt's face flashed in her mind, but she pushed the thought of him aside. He wasn't like William, but he also wasn't interested in her. Wyatt didn't seem interested in anything beyond getting her out of his hair so he could avoid her family's drama.

He'd always hated her family and their twisted dynamics—not that *his* upbringing was without its problems. Yet he hardly ever spoke of his time in the foster care system or the few years he'd spent with his real parents. In fact, in all the time they had spent dating, he'd only spoken to her once about it—and it was merely that he was thankful for what Mrs. and Mr. Fitz had done for him. It was just one of those things they skirted around, each of them fearing what the other would say or the memories it would bring to the surface. Some wounds just didn't need to be exposed.

If only she could say the same of having to deal with William Poe.

William glanced back at her and had a scowl on his face. "Don't bring my wife into this, any of this. She doesn't deserve to be hurt just because your sister is angry."

"My sister isn't angry. And there are worse things that would hurt her far more than my sister's feelings. How about the fact that you screw anything that walks?"

"You don't know what you're talking about, Gwen." He said her name like it left a bitter aftertaste.

She didn't care.

"When was the last time you saw Bianca?"

"What?" He looked confused. "Why?"

"Don't worry about it." She smiled, the motion dangerous. "When was the last time you saw her?"

He shrugged. "I don't know. Last week sometime?"

"Where?"

He stared at her as though he was the one trying to read her now. "At her clinic. Why? What are you trying to get at? Is she missing or something?"

She stood in silence, not ready to say the words and acknowledge the reality of where Bianca currently rested.

The back door opened and William's wife, Monica, walked out with a dishtowel in her hand. Her dark hair was pulled back in a small, stylish chignon that made her look every bit the high-end antiques shop owner that she was. Over the years Gwen had gone into Monica's shop, picking up odds and ends, pieces for the ranch, and once in a while even selling things her family didn't need. Before everything with Bianca, she had thought the woman a friend, but thanks to her sister and her sister's secrets, she had let their friendship dissolve out of fear she would be caught in the middle.

Gwen sucked in a breath as she realized how, in this moment, that was exactly where she was.

"Hi, Gwen. How're you doing?" Monica asked, sending her a smile that made guilt roil within her.

Gwen smiled. She could tell her right now.

"Hi, Monica. I'm okay. You?" she asked, trying to sound as though she didn't have a war raging within her.

"Good," Monica said, with a look that spoke of her confusion at why exactly Gwen was standing in her driveway and talking to her husband. "Do you want to come in and have a cup of coffee?" She glanced at Gwen's clothes and added, "If you want you could come in and get cleaned up? What have you been up to?"

Gwen looked down at herself and realized why the woman was offering. Her shirt was sprinkled with bits of hay and her shoes were covered in the filth of the compost pile. She must have looked like a mess to them, but no matter how bad she looked on the outside it was nothing to the mess she was within.

"No. No, I'm fine," she said, trying to keep her embarrassment from seeping into her voice. "I was just going."

"Is there something I can help you with?" Monica asked, looking to William as though she were trying to get a clearer picture.

"No, honey, she's fine. Just had a question about the Widow Maker's taxes, isn't that right, Gwen?" he said, leading her into the answers he wanted.

As much as she wanted to tell him to pound sand, and tell Monica why she was really here, she bit her tongue. She hadn't gotten the answers she needed from William—and if she started a war between him and his wife, she doubted she ever would. But his day was coming. William would pay for the way he treated women—and her sister.

Gwen nodded. "I'll stop by your office sometime soon. I still have a few more questions."

William gave Monica a quick peck on her cheek, like he hadn't been kissing Gwen's sister all that long ago. It made a feeling of sickness rise within her.

Gwen turned away, unable to stomach watching the vile man any longer.

"Have a great day, Gwen," Monica called from behind her. "And stop by the shop sometime. I have some new things I think you'd love!"

Monica sounded excited, and it made the hatred Gwen felt for William even more palpable. Monica didn't deserve to be treated the way William treated her—even if she didn't know it.

Gwen got into the truck and reversed down the driveway. As she stopped near the bottom, in the distance she could make out the profile of Wyatt's squad car returning from Kalispell. He approached her truck, then slowed down and pulled to a stop beside her. He frowned as he looked at her.

"What are you doing at the Poes'?" he asked, glancing up toward the house. His face contorted with disgust as though he held the same opinion of William Poe she did—but then again, William had a reputation. "You know William? How well?" He gave her a questioning look.

Wait. Did he think she was here to see William for *that*? She blanched at the thought.

"No. I came here…" she started, but if she told him why she was here she would have to tell him about Bianca's relationship with William. If she didn't he would assume she was the one sleeping with William. Both options made her want to turn and run.

She stopped. There was no right answer here. "I was just about to run to take a shower."

The disgusted look on Wyatt's face disappeared and she caught a glimpse of a naughty smile. Was he thinking of her in the shower? No. She must have had it all wrong. He was probably just glad she was leaving the Poes'.

"Are you going home?" he asked.

She glanced down at her pants and realized that if she went home, her mother would likely be waiting to barrage her with a litany of questions about Bianca and what she and Wyatt were working on. Gwen didn't know if she was ready to face her mother. Not yet anyway.

"I…uh…" she stammered. "My mother is probably up."

"It's almost noon." He glanced toward his dashboard, where there must have been a clock.

"She hit the bars again last night. Didn't come home at closing time. Nights like that, she normally comes rolling in about the time the man she went home with wakes up and finds her in his bed."

Wyatt's face turned to stone. In fact, that stoic look was the one he always had when it came to her family—and she hated it. It was almost as though they embarrassed him, or was it that he pitied her because of them? Either way, it made her want to talk about anything else.

"If you like," he said, "you're welcome to come to my place and get cleaned up. I have a T-shirt or two that might fit you."

His offer came as a shock. Did he really mean to invite her over? She tried not to read too much into his invitation. No doubt he was just trying to be nice and she'd just heard what she wanted to when she picked up the hint of something more in his voice.

Wait. Did she want him to come on to her?

She chuckled. Of course she did. Who didn't want to be thought of as beautiful?

She'd been lonely for so long. Her relationships in recent years had been nothing more than surface-level attractions—nights spent fulfilling her need to be touched and to feel another body against hers. It would have felt good to have him want her, to have him think of her as something more than the girl who'd once broken his heart.

When she'd ended their relationship, she'd felt justified in her decision. Life had been pulling them in different directions. He wanted to leave and go to NYU to escape the sucking maw of ranch life while she was restricted by her mother's disapproval. After her father's death, her mother hated the Fitzgeralds because of their association with what Gwen had come to realize was really the end of her mother's life. He had to go and she had to stay—it wasn't a gap that could be bridged.

Yet when life hadn't turned out to be as glamorous as Wyatt had planned in the big city, he had returned home. At the time, Gwen had thought about seeking him out to see if the old feelings were still there, but at the last minute she had thought better of it. Some kinds of pain you could never heal or apologize enough for—especially when her actions had caused her just as much agony.

She looked into his soft brown eyes and he

smiled. Or maybe she had been wrong. Maybe it was her fear of being rejected for the hurt she had caused that was really holding her back. Maybe he had grown past the pain she had inflicted when they'd been young and, in her case, stupid.

"So?" he asked, pulling her from her thoughts. "If you don't want to come back to my place to clean up, I totally understand. I was just thinking... Well, I was hoping to get in touch with the crime lab to see if they found anything, and then maybe work on the library lead. Thought it could save us both some time and a few trips, but it's completely up to you."

He was rambling.

The realization made her chest ache. Seeing him like that made some of the feelings she thought she'd buried rise to the surface.

He had always been a good man, and nothing if not a gentleman. Of course his offer had come from a place of sincerity and not some player's attempt at getting her to land in his bed.

"All right," she said with a nod. "I'll follow you back."

He moved to speak, but stopped and instead

dipped his head and motioned for her to follow him home.

She pressed down on the pickup's gas pedal and made it rumble with life. Though she should have been thinking of nothing but Bianca and their investigation, as she pushed the truck forward, all she could think of was how glad she was to find Wyatt back in her life.

Chapter Six

Some of the snow had started to melt and dirt patches were showing through as Gwen and Wyatt drove down the winding, bumpy road that led to his trailer at Dunrovin. She could see his place in the distance, a single wreath on the door—a single man's attempt at Christmas cheer.

She was looking forward to going inside and seeing what his life had become, but at the same time she was nervous. If one thing led to another, she didn't know how she would react. Or what it would be like if nothing happened. She wasn't sure which order of possible events disappointed her more.

She ran her finger over her lips, imagining his kiss. He had been a good kisser in high school. She could only imagine what he would be like now, ten years and what was probably dozens of women later. The thought of him with another woman made her skin prickle with jealousy. She tried to ignore the sensation. It was crazy to feel that way about him and what he chose to do. She had no claim on him.

He pulled to a stop in front of his trailer. The little tan box wasn't anything like the house she had imagined he would end up in—or rather, when she'd been imagining back in high school, the house *they* would have ended up living in together. In her mind's eye, she had once pegged them for living the American dream: two kids, a dog and a white picket fence.

She chuckled as she got out of the truck. How naive she had once been. Life wasn't some dream. She had been stupid to think it could be. Life was simply a constant battle between wants and needs. And here in Montana, in a world where winter and Mother Nature seemed to constantly reign, needs were all that mattered.

"What are you laughing about?" he asked, waiting for her by the front of the truck.

She hadn't even realized she had been laughing at the thought, and his calling her out caught her off guard. "What?"

"You were laughing at something."

"Oh," she said, closing the door. "It was nothing."

"Huh," he said, sounding slightly disappointed that she refused to let him in on the joke. "I'll grab you a towel and some clean clothes. Maybe I have something that won't hang on you too much."

She followed him up the rickety wooden steps and into the trailer. She wasn't sure what she had expected, but the place was a bit of a shock. Everything was in order. When he took her coat, she noticed that even the coat closet was organized: on one side were all his black work jackets and from there everything was arranged by color. She walked into his living room. The room was simple: a flat screen on the wall above an electric stove and a leather couch at the room's heart.

There wasn't a single forgotten sock or speck of dust. In fact, it was almost a little too clean—which made her wonder if he was the kind who was so concentrated on his house that he forgot to leave it. Perhaps he had gone from the boy who wanted to escape the confines and trappings of ranch life to a man who wanted nothing more than to bask in the comfort of the ranching lifestyle. It struck her how much he may have changed from the boy she had once known.

He made his way through the dining room off the kitchen and into what must have been the master bedroom. She followed him to the door of the room but stopped, unsure of whether or not he wanted her to be in his domain. His bedroom was just as clean as the rest of the place, and his bed was made with a pink floral quilt that she had no doubt was handmade by his mother.

"I like the quilt," she said, leaning against the door frame as she motioned to the blanket.

"Huh?" He looked surprised by her talking, or maybe it was that he was just as uncomfortable as she was. "Oh, that? It's just a hand-me-down. My mother had it forever and then made herself a new one." He chuckled. "It may be pink, but I'm enough of a man not to be afraid to rock it. Until now, no one ever really saw it anyways."

She could have sworn she saw the color rise in his cheeks when he mentioned his bedroom activities, or lack thereof.

"It's okay, I'm pretty sure I still have *Star Wars* sheets from when I was a kid. Heck, I still use my twin-size bed." She laughed as she tried to make him feel better.

His face lit up. "Oh, I remember that old thing. That bed was a bit creaky when we were together. I can't believe you still have it." He laughed, but then stopped abruptly as though he had realized exactly what they were talking about. "I mean, I would have thought you'd have gotten rid of it by now."

"Why get rid of a good thing?" As the words left her, she realized the other meaning they held and she wished she could reel them back in. Yet, there was no coming back from putting her foot that deeply into her mouth.

"That's... I didn't mean..." she said, struggling to stop the light from going completely out of his eyes. She had liked seeing him smile, seeing him light up when they were talking about the past. She hated herself for what she had done to him, regardless of her reasons at the time—everything going on with her family, their loss and the hatred her mother carried toward him had seemed like things they would never be able to overcome if they wanted to make a life together. Even then, she had known that true love meant sometimes sacrificing the things she held dearest—even if that meant stopping the relationship so that neither of them would have to go through a lifetime of pain. He had de-

served to have a life filled with happiness—
and he still did.

He waved her off. "It's fine. I'm sure you
were just talking about that old mattress."

She could hear the hurt in his tone.

"I really was. I…I'm sorry about the past,
Wyatt. About what happened. You know…
when we were younger. I was stupid. I just
thought the divide between our families was
too big and I was trying to protect us both.
Who knows, maybe I just watched too much
Romeo and Juliet or something."

"You weren't stupid," he said, his voice
quiet with what she assumed was discomfort
at having this conversation. "You did what you
thought you had to do. I get it. You don't need
to explain yourself to me. What happened,
happened. There's no going back." There was
a finality in the way he said the words, and it
made the air thick between them.

"You're right. There's no going back," she
said, trying to make it sound soft and repen-
tant, and she hoped that he could hear the
apology in her words. "But there is always
moving forward."

"I'm truly sorry about Bianca," he said.

He was right to assume she had been talking about the investigation and her sister. Bi-

anca should have been who she was talking about. Her sister's death should have been consuming all her thoughts and actions. Yet, standing here by Wyatt's bedroom and looking at his warm bed, her mind moved to the wants she had been repressing for so long.

"Thanks, I appreciate it. I do." She stepped into his bedroom and moved close to him, so close she could feel the warmth radiating off his body. "But I wasn't talking about Bianca."

He took in a long breath as he stared at her. She had no idea what he could possibly be thinking. All she could think about was how weightless she felt as she looked into his eyes and the way her chest clenched with want. She hadn't been this nervous around a man in long time.

She stepped closer, until she brushed against the thick brown polyester of his uniform shirt and her belly bumped against his utility belt. He was just a bit taller than she had remembered. She looked down at his pants, the action of looking at him feeling even naughtier when she thought about it, and heat rose in her cheeks.

Instead of laughing at her embarrassment, he put his hands on her shoulders. His thumbs made those familiar circles she had thought she hated, but now she leaned into his touch, wanting more. It felt good to be touched by him…so good.

She looked up. There was nothing but him. His eyes. The fine crow's-feet that sat at their corners. The smooth skin of his freshly shaven face. His pink, full lips were damp. He must have just licked them.

The thought made her body quiver to life. Her center grew heavy with want and the desire for his hands to move from her shoulders. For him to rub those little circles he liked so much in darker, more forbidden places.

She wanted to speak, to tell him how badly she wanted him. Yet the words caught in her throat, and before she had the chance, he dropped his hands from her and turned away.

No. He couldn't.

Was he rejecting her? Didn't he want her? *This?*

She moved to reach for him, but stopped. If he didn't want her, it was his choice. He had every right to refuse her.

Reality and the disappointment that came with it poured in from all sides as he walked across the bedroom and, opening the linen closet, grabbed a towel.

"Here," he said, handing the towel to her.

Her hands shook as she took it. She didn't know what to say or how to cover her embarrassment and graciously accept the fact that he no longer wanted her in the same way she wanted him.

"I...er... Thanks," she said, but as soon as the words were out of her, she turned and nearly sprinted for the bathroom that was connected to the room.

She closed the door behind her harder than she intended, and the harsh sound reverberated through the room, echoing the pain in her chest.

She was such an idiot. Of course he didn't want her like she wanted him. They'd only been speaking to each other for a day. Up until then, they had treated each other like they were invisible. What had happened in the past, and the feelings it had generated, couldn't vanish overnight.

Then again, she'd never forgotten him. More nights than she could count, he was the last person on her mind before she slipped away to sleep. And during long days on the ranch baling hay or moving the cattle, she would let her thoughts wander...always to him and the what-ifs. What if she hadn't let him go? What if they had stayed together?

Would they have stayed in Mystery, or would they have run away from this place? He'd run, but if she had gone with him, how different would their lives have been?

She thought of the way he had just looked at her. His look hadn't been indifferent, he hadn't seemed put off by her or her move toward him, but it hadn't been the look of a man who loved her either.

She sighed.

Not for the first time, she was letting her emotions run away with her. She couldn't move this fast.

She tried to stop chastising herself. She couldn't regret the action she had taken. It was brave to follow her heart, even if it had been foolish. If she hadn't tried, she wouldn't have known his true feelings—or that he wasn't interested.

She flipped on the faucet in the shower and let the water run until steam poured from behind the glass. She was fine. It would be fine. It wasn't like she had completely thrown herself at him. If she was careful, she could make it seem like nothing. She could bounce back from this. She had to. She had to face him again.

They had work to do.

With a renewed sense of spirit, she stepped into the shower. It was so hot that it made the skin of her back tingle and burn, but she didn't turn down the heat. She wanted—no, needed—to feel the pain. The stinging needles reminded her that things could be so much worse. She was alive. Unlike Bianca.

She put her hands on the tile of the shower wall. It was cold against her hot hands. In here, away from the prying eyes of the world, she let the tears come as the crazy mixture of emotions she'd been trying to hold back finally bubbled to the surface. Here, she didn't have to hide.

Heaving sobs rattled through her body and she sank to the warmed floor. The water swirled down the drain as it mixed with her tears.

Screw being strong. Screw the world for what it had done to her sister—and screw it for continuing to break her down.

She shouldn't have felt sorry for herself, but she couldn't help it. Every time she turned around, it was as if the world was throwing another curveball her way. Just as soon as she had dealt with one thing, it was always like there was another thing coming.

She was just so dang tired.

Leaning against the tile, she let her tears fall.

"Gwen?" Wyatt called from behind the door. "Are you okay?"

She wasn't, but she wasn't about to tell him. "Fine. I'm fine." She turned off the water and stepped out of the shower, wrapping herself in the oversize towel he'd given her.

There was a long pause. "I, uh, got you some clean clothes. Do you want me to set them outside the door here?"

She opened the bathroom door, carefully holding her towel in place. "I'll take them," she said, as a drip of water slipped down her leg and pooled on the floor.

Wyatt looked at her and his eyes widened. His gaze moved down her body to the puddle on his floor.

"You're dripping." He moved toward her, so close that they were nearly touching. Instead of continuing past her, he stopped and their eyes met.

Her breath hitched. Maybe she had gotten it wrong. Maybe he did want her. Maybe he'd been acting the gentleman by turning her away before.

He leaned in and his lips met hers. He smelled like the compost pile and hay, but she didn't care as he pulled her into his arms.

She let go of her towel, letting it be held by their bodies as she wrapped her arms around his neck and ran her fingers through his hair.

His lips moved over hers, then she sucked and ran the tip of her tongue over his skin. He tasted like peppermint gum and sweat, just as he had when they were younger. Yet his kiss was not the same. It was the kiss of a man—a man who knew exactly what he wanted.

He pushed her body against the wall and lifted her hands over her head. The radio on his utility belt pressed hard against her and, as he noticed her discomfort, he unclasped the belt and let it fall to the floor at their feet.

He traced the line of her jaw, kissing the places where his fingers had touched. Each time his fingers slipped lower on her skin, down her neck and onto her collarbone. He licked and sucked the beads of water from her skin, and for a second she wondered if he could taste the salt from her tears.

She pulled her hands down and took hold of the buttons on his uniform, stopping him from going any lower. She wanted him. His touch. His lips upon her skin. But she'd envisioned this moment so many times, so many nights when she'd been lying alone in her bed and thinking about what could have been, that she wanted to savor this moment and make it last.

"You need a shower," she said with a coy grin.

As though she had reeled him back to reality, he stopped and looked down at his shirt. He chuckled as he must have realized the state he was in.

"Sorry," he said, pulling back from her.

Her towel slipped and she moved to grab it, but stopped and let it fall to the floor atop his utility belt.

"There's nothing to be sorry for," she said, her voice high and airy with lust.

She slipped the buttons free as he stared at her body. Under her fingertips, she could feel the erratic beating of his heart and his short, choppy breaths as her hands worked lower. She pulled his shirt from him and dropped it to the floor away from her towel.

Bits of hay were still stuck to his tank top from his digging through the compost pile. She pulled a piece from his shirt. He was such a good man. How could she have ever let him go?

She had regretted her decision in the past, but never more than right now. If she had just followed her heart and not her head or the pressures of the people around her, she could have been with him all these years. They had missed so much time together all because she had made a major miscalculation.

There was only moving forward.

She reached down and unbuttoned his pants. He took her hand and lifted them to his lips and kissed them.

"Are you sure?" he asked, kissing the inside of her palm. "Are you positive that you want to take things down this road again?"

"I am sure, but are you?" She wrapped her free hand around his neck and leaned back against the wall, letting him glimpse her in full glory.

She wasn't playing fair and she knew it, but she didn't care. All was fair in love and war. Not that she loved him.

No. Definitely not love.

Probably.

She pushed the thought from her mind as she led him to the shower and stripped off his shirt. There was a piece of hay in the sparse hair that adorned the center of his chest. She liked a man with a little brown sugar. As she pulled the hay off him, she ran her fingers through the little patch and giggled.

"What's so funny?" he asked, a grin on his sexy face.

"Nothing. It's just a little thicker than the last time I saw it." She pulled at the single gray hair that was mixed in the patch. "And it looks like you are starting to get a little salt in the pepper."

"It's not gray," he said, looking down at his chest and pulling at the hair. "That is summer blond, baby."

She laughed, the sound warming her from the inside out.

How she had missed him.

She turned the water on in the shower as he slipped his pants off. He stood there in his boxer briefs, looking at her as she turned back around.

"Did anyone ever tell you how beautiful you are?"

She waved him off. As much as she loved hearing the compliment, she didn't quite know how to respond.

"No, really. And if you turn around again…" He leaned around, trying to catch another glimpse of her behind.

"What?" she said, playfully turning away from him.

He gave her an impish grin. "Do you really want to find out?"

She giggled and stepped into the shower, pulling the curtain just far enough closed that it covered her body, but she could see out. "Only if you meet me in here."

Just when she thought he couldn't get any hotter, his impish grin grew into a full smile, making a dimple appear in his right cheek. He reached down and slipped his fingers under the edge of his underwear and wiggled his hips.

It felt so good to see him being playful.

"I like it. Dance for me, baby," she teased.

He laughed as he swung his hips in a full circle and lowered his underwear, exposing the edge of his pubic hair.

"Lower…"

"How low?" he said, continuing to swing his hips.

"All the way."

He raised his brow and stopped dancing. He paused for a minute, then pulled the boxers down his legs and stepped out of them.

She sucked in a breath as she looked at all of him. She had felt him against her, but she hadn't quite expected what faced her.

He stepped into the shower and pulled her

back into his arms. The water splashed on him, creating rivulets that streamed down his body. It was strange, but she couldn't help but think that being in his arms was the one place where she truly belonged.

They let the water run over their bodies as he pushed her against the water-warmed tile of the shower wall and kissed her. He tasted savory in all the right ways.

He traced her curves with his fingers until he found his way to her backside. He cupped it, and his kiss moved deeper, harder with want. His hunger for her made every inch of her body scream to be touched, to be felt and tasted. She opened her legs and pulled him closer to her, so close she could feel all of him against her.

The sensation of him against her wet skin made her prickle to life. Every dream she had envisioned and every thought she'd had about this time with him was nothing in comparison to the reality of feeling him between her thighs.

He leaned down, pulling her nipple into his mouth and making a sucking noise. She loved that noise, the pop of his mouth on her sensitive nub. She moaned his name and his kiss hardened on her.

She could live in this moment forever.

There was the sound of the phone ringing somewhere from beneath the pile of clothes just outside the shower. She tried to ignore it, but the Gary Allan song "Get Off on the Pain" continued to sound, and it pulled her from her euphoria.

"Is...is that your phone?" she said, drunk with want.

"Huh?" He stopped kissing her and she immediately regretted having spoken.

"Your phone."

It stopped ringing. For a moment they stood there in silence, just letting the water rush over them. Then the phone started ringing again, persistent with its need to be answered.

"Son of a—"

"What?"

"It's probably the medical examiner. He promised he would call." He gave her a look that said he had to take the call.

She was immediately brought back to reality. Their stolen moment was over... No matter how badly she wanted to fall into the daydream, the nightmare of the real world waited.

Chapter Seven

He wasn't sure how he'd gotten so lucky to find himself alone with her in the shower, but he would give just about anything to get back in and not have his phone ring. He'd never thought of himself as unlucky, but when he'd been forced to step away from her, he couldn't help but think the universe had it out for him.

He pulled the device from his utility belt as it sounded again. "Deputy Fitzgerald," he answered, irritation filling in his voice.

"Fitz, how goes it?" the medical examiner asked, either ignoring or completely oblivious to his tone.

Wyatt looked at Gwen, who had already turned off the shower and wrapped her body back in the towel he had watched hit the floor only minutes before. He walked to the rack and grabbed his own towel, wrapping it around his waist as modesty dictated, though his body wanted something entirely different.

He could have sworn a look of disappointment swept over her face, but he couldn't be sure. Then again, she had been the one who had tried to seduce him—though admittedly she didn't have to try too hard. It had taken all of his willpower to turn her away the first time because he had thought her too raw from grief to make a good decision about their being together. But the second time, when she dropped that towel…well, he couldn't say no. A man could only resist and listen to his head so much before his body and its desires took over.

"Fitz?" the woman asked.

"Yeah, so… Find anything?" He forced himself to look away from Gwen and the perfect curves of her body. With a body like that, round and soft in all the right places, there was no way he could pay attention to the woman on the other end of the phone.

Though he tried to look away, he could still see her in the mirror, bending over and running the edge of her towel down her legs.

Dang, she was so flipping sexy.

He left the bathroom and gently pulled

the door shut behind him so he wouldn't be tempted to look back. He had to focus.

"The syringe you brought us was quite helpful. Upon closer inspection, we did manage to find a small mark on her neck that was consistent with the mark that would be made by a large gauge needle."

"Did you test the syringe's contents?"

"That's really why I was calling." The woman paused. "We found something interesting. Something that I didn't even know we tested for, to be honest. Have you ever heard of the drug Beuthanasia?"

"What?" he asked, struggling to imagine what exactly the woman was talking about.

"Beuthanasia, it's used on animals...to put them to down."

"Are you kidding me?"

The woman clicked her tongue against her teeth. "Once my techs learned about the syringe and the victim's job, it was one of the next chemical compounds that they tested for. If it wasn't for them and their ability to put two and two together, I can't say we would have figured out exactly what killed her. With the amount of phenytoin and pentobarbital in her system, I can say that without a doubt it was what killed her."

"Who has access to it?" Wyatt asked.

"Well," the medical examiner started, "anyone who is registered with the DEA has access. They can order the drug, but they have to have a good record-keeping system. Actually, most veterinarians keep the drug on hand—especially the large-animal vets who may be called to a scene in which they can't transport a hurt animal and have to humanely end its life."

"So it could have been *Bianca's* medication?"

"Certainly… She was a vet, correct?"

"Is there any way to track where the drug could have come from? You know, which vial or something?" Wyatt asked.

The woman snorted into the phone. "No. We aren't some crime show. It's not something that's DNA based. The solution from one company is pretty much the same as the solution from another company. And truthfully, not knowing much about veterinarian medicine, I would assume there isn't a whole lot of diversity as far as who would carry and distribute the medicine."

"Huh. Okay. Did you manage to pull any prints from the syringe?"

He could almost imagine the lady shaking

her head. "Unfortunately, due to its condition, we couldn't pull any full prints that would be usable. However, the partial prints appeared to have a ridge pattern that wasn't that of your vic—ruling out any possibility that she may have killed herself."

"You are sure that it was the implement used in her death?"

"You're the one who would have to prove it in court, but thanks to the size of the needle and the size of the mark on your vic's neck, added to the fact that it was filled with the same chemical that killed her, I'd say you'd be more than likely to prove that it was what killed her beyond a reasonable doubt."

There had to be something he could use here. Maybe even something that could point him in the direction of who wanted Bianca dead—and why.

"Thanks for the information. I appreciate it. And, hey, if you find out anything else about this med, or about her death, please let me know. I'm at a bit of a loss with this one. Few known enemies and she was pretty well liked within the community."

"You're welcome. I'll let you know if I run across anything more," the medical examiner said.

He hung up the phone. From inside the bathroom, he could hear Gwen's footsteps as she moved around the room.

He set the phone down on his dresser and moved toward the door, but stopped at taking the handle. Undoubtedly, she would want to know what the examiner had found, but he wasn't sure that he wanted to tell her. Not yet. Not when they could finish what they started.

The handle turned in his hand and he let go.

Gwen opened the door. She was wearing the Yankees T-shirt that he had kept from his very limited days attending NYU. That shirt was about the only thing, besides maybe the baseball games and the food, that he'd really enjoyed in the monstrously huge city.

"You look cute," he said, putting his hands on the top of her hips and leaning back to take her in completely.

She stepped out of his hands, but the movement wasn't out of rejection. Rather, thanks to the faint pinkness in her cheeks, he assumed it was out of embarrassment. Was she upset about the choice she had made in the bathroom?

For him, what had just happened would probably go down in the books. He had loved it. It had been the first *real* thing that had happened in a long time. He was always working and moving. It was just an endless, habitual cycle that he had come to accept was his life—until yesterday and the moment he had seen her standing in the doorway in her red flannel nightgown.

That was the moment he'd sparked back to life. And he would forever be thankful for having her back in his world—it was just too bad it had to come under some terrible circumstances. If only he had listened to Bianca one of the million times she had tried to tell him to go after her sister, he could have come back to life a long time ago.

Or maybe he wouldn't have fallen into the trap of complacency.

"Who was that?" she asked, looking at him with the raise of her brow.

"Just some girl," he said, almost teasing as he tried to put off having to tell her what he'd found out.

"Oh, yeah?" From her tone, it wasn't just an innocent question; there was almost a fleck of jealousy.

He had to have been wrong. There was nothing for her to be jealous about.

He must have misread her. He was making something out of nothing, he'd probably heard something in her voice that wasn't even there. Regardless, their moment was over. He moved to his closet and pulled out a fresh uniform shirt and pants.

"That," he said, motioning to the cell phone on his dresser, "was the medical examiner. She was calling about your sister."

Her jaw went slack and her questioning expression disappeared. "What did she say?"

"You were right about the syringe and its tie to the case. It was filled with a compound they use for euthanizing animals. Someone ended up using it on your sister." He tried to say the words slowly, so each syllable wouldn't come as a slap to the face, but there was little he could do to lessen the fact that her sister really had been murdered.

Her gaze fell. Thankfully, unlike when he'd first told her of Bianca's death at the Widow Maker, she didn't sink to the floor.

"What does it mean for the case?" she asked, the words coming so slow it was like each was its own sentence.

"It means that this just became an official homicide investigation."

She leaned against the wall, trying to regain her balance.

"Are you okay?" he asked, throwing his

clothes over his arm as he moved toward her. When he got close she turned away, hiding her face.

"I'm fine," she said, but she walked out the door of his bedroom, closing it in her wake before he could say anything else.

He grumbled. Women were so complicated. He loved them, but, man, sometimes they were like a giant puzzle. Just when he thought he had gotten something figured out, another piece went missing.

He threw on his clothes and utility belt and slipped his phone into his pocket. Gwen was sitting at the island in his kitchen. She'd poured herself a glass of water and, as he approached, she was running her finger around its edges.

The sight of her there, looking broken-hearted, pulled at him. The first time he'd seen her looking like that had been the day she had learned about her father's death. Why did he always seem to come to her in moments of disaster? Was he her personal angel of death?

If he was, it was no wonder she was always pushing him away—that is, until they had been in his bathroom. His body tingled with unreleased desire, but he forced himself to ignore the sensation.

That had been a onetime thing. Heck. It had barely even been a thing. They had only seen each other naked. Though, it had been very, very naked and a bit more than simply just seeing. He thought of her pulling him between her thighs. At the thought, he could almost feel the heat of her again. She'd been hot, so hot. At sixteen, he had dreamed of being there—both of them naked and her body begging for him.

He snorted as he thought of how, no matter how old they were, or their situations, life always got in the way.

He stepped around the island and stood in front of her. "I know you said you're doing fine, but you know, you can talk to me about this…about *anything*." He motioned toward the bedroom. Not that he was exactly sure that he wanted to talk about what had happened in there, but he didn't want to let it go either—not if there was a way he could somehow make sense of what she wanted.

She didn't look where he motioned, almost as if she was purposefully ignoring his reference. "I…" She sighed, taking a moment. "Look, I'm sorry. For…*that*. You know, in the bathroom. I just…I don't know. If you have a girlfriend or something…I didn't have any business acting like that. Not that I didn't like it, but…" She stumbled over her words.

So that had been her problem? She thought he was dating someone? The thought made him laugh out loud. Sure, he'd dated, but none of them had ever compared to the memory of her.

He raised his hands from the counter, an action almost like that of a person surrendering. "Whoa. Stop. Babe." As he said the pet name, he wished he could have pulled it back. In the light of the kitchen, and with them both dressed, it just sounded out of place and awkward. "Gwen, I don't know why you'd think I have a girlfriend. I haven't had one in a long time." Her face brightened and some of the light seemed to return to her eyes.

"No girlfriend. That's *good*." She said the word as if she wasn't sure if it really was a good or bad thing. "But why…"

"I get it. I should have just said it was the medical examiner," he said, trying to stop the hatchet from falling before he had a chance to escape its blade. "Teasing you was a bad idea."

The brightness in her eyes once again disappeared.

"Yeah, it was," she said, standing up and

making the kitchen stool squeak against the floor. "Look, let's just go. We got a much-needed piece of the puzzle. I knew she wouldn't hurt herself. But now we need to find out who was behind her death."

He was thankful that she had changed the subject, but with the change he could also feel the emotional distance between them shift and widen.

"Let's go to the library," she continued. "Let's look more into the email and see if they have anything that could point us in the direction of who wrote it."

The library was a great next step, especially when she had been teasing him in the shower.

"About what happened in there—" He again motioned toward the bathroom, but she turned around and stopped him with a wave of her hand.

"What happened back there... It was great. I wanted it. You wanted it. But it can't be. Bianca and this investigation need to come first. I don't have the emotional space to have anything more in my life."

He opened his mouth to speak, but she interrupted him. "Do you remember when you once told me a dead-end road only needs to be driven once? Well, we both know this thing between us is a dead end. Let's just stop it before we have the chance to make the same mistake twice. Let's save us both the heartbreak."

GWEN LOOKED OUT the car window as they made their way down Main Street past the late-1800s brick buildings that lined both sides. The library was just up the road, a couple of storefronts down from Monica Poe's antiques shop, Secret Secondhand. It hadn't been a long car ride, but the silence between Gwen and Wyatt had made it seem like a marathon drive.

She hadn't meant to confront him about the phone call when he'd said it was a woman—she wasn't unhinged or possessive. He could talk to whomever, whenever he wanted. She held no claim, and what claim she had once had she'd willingly given up a long time ago.

Then again, maybe if she played her cards right she could get back in his good graces—but being jealous wasn't a good start.

Yet he had ended their time so abruptly and left the bathroom, and then the way he had teased her... He had made it seem like something more than just the medical examiner. So what else was she supposed to think? Men only acted like that when they were trying to hide something. That was something she knew all too much about, thanks to a handful of relationships that always ended with secrets and lies—not that she had really cared. If anything, she had always been called cold thanks to her general state of indifference toward men and the choices they made—at least men who weren't Wyatt.

Was it possible that she didn't care about what other men did because the only man she really wanted was Wyatt?

She glanced over at him as he stared out at the road. He had on a pair of aviators that perfectly accented his uniform. Everything about him was all business—and was one heck of a turn-on.

Yet she'd made her choice and pushed him away. It was just so much easier not to care—emotions were messy and she already had enough of that kind of thing on her hands. If she opened herself up, and listened to the desires that whispered through her, she would only get hurt. Her life and her heart had already been shattered with Bianca's death—if he hurt her, there would be nothing left.

He pulled the squad car into a parking spot.

Coming around to her side, he opened the door without a word and waited for her to step out.

"Thanks," she said as he closed the door behind her.

He grumbled something unintelligible as he turned away and made his way up to the front doors of the library. She followed behind him, slowly picking her way through patches of ice in an attempt to give him his space.

If this was what it was going to be like, working with him and his hurt ego, she wasn't sure it was something she could handle. Then again, she didn't have any other options. He was the only one investigating her sister's death. Because Mystery was so small, even though it was now a homicide investigation, there was no one else to turn to and no one else who could have possibly cared as much as he did.

He would just have to get over it. They had both made the mistake of falling into each other's arms. Sure, she had been the one to push it forward, but it had been done in a moment of weakness. All she had wanted was to feel again. It had been spontaneous and poorly thought out. There were so many reasons they shouldn't be anything more than friends—or rather, colleagues. Right now, they needed to concentrate on the investigation. Then maybe they could try again, or at least work on creating a friendship.

He opened the front door and waited for her to catch up. Even slightly annoyed with him, and trying to ignore her feelings, she couldn't help appreciating the fact that, regardless of his mood or the events of the day, he was always a gentleman. It was a lost art, and something she had assumed would have been taken from him after his days in the city. Yet, if anything, he was even more of a gentleman than she had remembered.

She wished she could just ask him all the questions she had, but she couldn't—not now. There was no question of whether or not she liked him, everyone who knew Wyatt as anything more than a sheriff's deputy liked him. He was a good man. A man who was built on strong morals and principles, a man's man— actually, he checked every box on the husband-material list.

She pushed the thought from her mind as she glanced up into his face, but he looked away as she moved past him and into the library. She couldn't think about him like this, there was no point to it. She needed to focus.

She needed to find justice for Bianca—not a bedroom partner.

As the library's door slid shut behind them, the scent of old books wafted toward her. She loved that smell—the odor of wood pulp, ink, glue and dreams of both authors and readers. This one small building, this little brick outcrop in a town of shadowy secrets, had always been her mecca.

They made their way to the front desk, where the librarian was nose-deep in a book. She didn't look up until Wyatt cleared his throat.

The woman jerked, glancing up from behind her reading glasses. "Oh, hi, sorry," she said, lifting the book like it was more than enough of an excuse for her obliviousness.

"Completely understand, Frannie," Wyatt said, with an appreciative nod to her love of reading.

Dang it. Did the man have to be perfect all the time? Didn't he know that Gwen was trying to find reasons *not* to like him?

"I didn't see you standing there, Wyatt," Frannie said with a smile as she gave them both an acknowledging tip of the head. "'You can never get a cup of tea large enough or a book long enough to suit me.'"

"C. S. Lewis quote?" Gwen asked.

Frannie's smile widened. "A fellow bibliophile, I love it. I can't say that I've ever been able to understand why more people don't love books." The librarian slipped a bookmark between the pages and laid the book on the counter.

"They're worlds where we can escape. We can live a thousand lives in the pages, or we can live merely the one we are given—I'll take a thousand lives every time," Wyatt said with a light chuckle.

Gwen could have sworn she had seen Frannie swoon.

"I...uh... Yes." The woman just stopped short of fanning herself. "Was there something I could help you two with?"

Gwen had seen Frannie at least a hundred times over the last few years, when Gwen would come to escape the confines of the ranch and find a book that could get her mind off whichever of her mother's antics she had been dealing with, but she'd never seen Frannie smile the way she did when she looked up at Wyatt.

"Actually, we were alerted to the fact that one of your computers may have been used in a crime. Would you mind if we asked you a few questions?" Wyatt leaned against the counter, taking a passive stance instead of his normal straight, shoulders back, no-nonsense officer stance. It was like he was trying to put the woman at ease, but Frannie kept looking back and forth between Gwen and Wyatt, so much so that Gwen felt out of place.

"If you don't mind," Gwen said, taking the woman's hint, "I'll excuse myself and go check out the computer bank. Is that okay?"

The woman nodded, almost a bit too fervently. "Help yourself. You know where the computers are, Gwen."

It came as a bit of a shock that the woman knew her name—it was certainly the first time that she had ever bothered to use it. Did her sudden friendliness have something to do with the fact that handsome Wyatt was there, or was it due to the fact that he was there in an official capacity as a deputy?

It was funny, but over the last day she had almost forgotten what and who Wyatt was to everyone else. He wasn't the silly boy from high school who had loved nothing more than AC/DC and laying in the back of his pickup on hot summer nights. No. To others he was the voice of authority, the man who came to their rescue in their moments of terror. He was their hero.

What would it have been like if she'd allowed him to be hers?

Ha. No. She could save herself.

The bank of computers was down a long set of stairs that creaked as she followed them into the belly of the building. The air grew a bit dank and earthy as she made her way into the basement. There was something about the smell that always made the hair on the back of her neck stand at attention. She was too old to be afraid of a smell, but there was just something about it that made it seem dangerous and foreboding.

She was tough, but for a moment she considered turning around and moving back up into the main library and the safety of the book stacks.

Whatever. Whoever had sent Bianca the threatening emails from this room wasn't still there waiting for her like some kind of bogeyman. They were definitely a monster, but it was possible they weren't responsible for killing Bianca. Maybe her sister had been a victim of merely being in the wrong place at the wrong time. *Or not.*

She sighed. She wished they had more to

work with. Right now it just seemed like there were so many more questions than answers, and she didn't see it changing at any point in the near future.

The computer lab was full of computers from the 1990s, complete with heavy-looking monitors and keyboards so ignored that several of them were thick with dust and she couldn't see their letters. The place was warm from the heat put off by the ancient machines and it hummed as the beasts struggled in what she was sure was their death throes.

There were only four computers up and running and, for a moment, she wondered which one the possible murderer had sat at. What had they had been thinking when they'd written Bianca the threat? Had they really meant to follow through with their plan? Was this the first time they'd threatened someone? Was it even the first time they had threatened her sister?

The room was nearly empty, except for the hanging industrial lights that buzzed as they looked down on her and the six desks that were lined against the dark, nearly black walls. She walked around the room, looking for anything that could possibly point in their suspect's direction, but there were no loose papers or notes scratched into the wooden desks.

The place was industrial. Whoever came down here, into what was a modern-day dungeon, had to have had a plan to kill her sister.

There was the sound of footsteps and the creak of the stairs. The eerie sound made her heart race and she looked up. Thankfully, it was just Wyatt.

"Did you find anything?" he asked as he walked into the hot room.

She shook her head. "What did the librarian know?"

Other than that she wanted to be in your pants? She snorted at the thought.

"What?" he asked, frowning.

"Oh, nothing. What did she tell you?"

He continued to stare at her like he was trying to read her, but she turned away, pretending to look around one of the desks. Just like the keyboards, it was covered in a thick layer of dust.

"She said there have been a lot of people in and out of the library lately, but she couldn't recall anyone asking to use the computers or seeing anyone come down here in the last few weeks."

The staircase that led to the basement was

out of view of the librarian's desk and, given the way she was buried in a book when they'd arrived, it didn't come as a surprise that the woman wouldn't have noticed someone coming or going from the depths. But Gwen was disappointed.

"What are we going to do, Wyatt?"

"It wasn't a completely wasted trip," Wyatt said as he ran his finger over one of the desks. He wiped the dirt from his finger on the leg of his pants, leaving a streak. "According to Frannie, she ran into Monica Poe when she was opening up her store this morning."

"And?"

"She was sporting a fresh black eye." He looked at Gwen with a raise of the brow. "Did you slug her when you were at her house?"

"What?" she asked, completely affronted by the question. "What are you talking about?"

"So *you* didn't hit her?" he asked.

"Absolutely not. Did she say I did?"

She and William's wife had barely spoken to each other before she'd left. And Monica most certainly hadn't had a black eye when Gwen left. If anything, they'd been more than cordial with each other.

Wyatt shook his head. "I was just wondering, why exactly were you up at the Poes' this morning? Did it have something to do with Monica? Or did it have something to do with William?"

Her stomach clenched. "I don't know what you're implying, Wyatt."

He glanced down at his pants and, noticing the streak of dirt he'd left, dusted it off. "I'm not implying anything, Gwen. You may or may not know this, but William Poe has a bit of a reputation when it comes to women. He has been with most of the single women in this town—and several who weren't single. At least that's the word on the street. No judgment, but I need want to know if you are or aren't sleeping with William Poe."

Her face turned hot with embarrassment. "I am aware of his reputation and I can barely stand being in the same town as him. I can't believe you think I'd have anything *like that* to do with a man like him."

"Look, you won't tell me why you were at the Poes' house this morning, and now Monica has a black eye...I have every right to question you." Wyatt leaned against a support beam near the room's center. "If you're into men like William, I think you were right in assuming we wouldn't be a good fit."

Her hand balled into a fist as she thought

of what he was implying and the kind of girl he thought she was.

"I don't have anything going on with that pig William Poe. I'd rather spend the rest of my life in a nunnery than have to spend one single second more with him. So you have nothing to worry about." She flexed her hands as she tried to control her temper. Wyatt wasn't wrong for reacting as he was. When she'd learned about Bianca and William, her reaction had been far more volatile...and filled with several expletives that she hadn't unleashed in years.

"And about Monica," she continued. "That woman deserves a medal, not a slug to the face, for putting up with a man like her husband."

"So you weren't, and have never, slept with him. Good." Some of the tightness in his features seemed to slip away. "But you still didn't answer my question about why you were there."

She sighed. "If I tell you, you have to promise to keep the information between us. Got it?"

He pushed away from the wall and looked over his shoulder like he was checking to make sure they were alone and out of the librarian's hearing distance. "I promise."

"*I* didn't sleep with him. But he and Bianca… They were having an affair."

Chapter Eight

That changed everything. Wyatt wasn't sure if he should be relieved or angry with Gwen. How could she have kept a secret of that magnitude from him for this long? She had to have known what implications it could have in their investigations.

"Why didn't you tell me this before?" he asked.

She dug the toe of her shoe into the concrete floor. "I don't think he had anything to do with her death. That's why I went to their house, to see exactly what he knew—and just to see his reaction. I had to."

"Did it ever occur to you that you could have compromised everything? If he's behind your sister's death, then you just showed our enemy our cards."

She looked up at him with wide eyes. "No. That's not it. That's not what I did. I swear."

"Then what were you thinking, Gwen?"

"Don't come at me like that," she said, anger filling her voice. "I didn't want to tell you about their affair because you were Bianca's friend. You can't tell me that something like this—her relationship with a married, piggish man—doesn't change your opinion of her. And if word of it got out…" She paused. "Now that she's gone, her reputation and our memories of her… That's all we have left."

He stood in silence, unsure of what to say. He wanted to make her feel better. He wanted to take her in his arms and tell her there were so many important things that mattered more than her sister's reputation in this small town. But then again, he could understand why she was so protective of her sister's honor.

He loved his brothers, Waylon, Rainier and Colter. He would protect them just like she protected her sister. Heck, once in the fifth grade, right after Rainier and Colter had been adopted, Wyatt had gotten in a fistfight on the school's playground. One close-minded little jerk had made the mistake of thinking he could make fun of them for being a different color.

He had taken the boy down, splitting his lip with one well-placed punch. But even though he had won the fight, it had done little to help the war he and his brothers had to face in the small town after word had spread that the two new Fitz boys were of Native American descent. In a rural town like Mystery, there would always be those people who hated those who were different.

And if word got out about how different, or immoral, Bianca's behavior had been in having an affair with a married man, it wouldn't just be Bianca's memory that could be impacted. Without a doubt, Gwen hadn't yet realized that the revelation could hurt her reputation as well. And it was more than possible that some self-righteous slob would think some kind of justice would need to be paid for Bianca's sinful actions—and that was where things could get dangerous for Gwen and her mother.

"Does your mom know about Bianca's relationship?"

Gwen shook her head.

At least they had one thing going for them. If Carla knew about it, it was more than likely she would spill the beans to the other barflies, and that would be a recipe for danger.

"You need to make sure she doesn't find out. No matter what," he continued. "I will keep this to myself. But you know we're going to have to look into him—and Monica. Do you think his wife knows about the relationship?"

"No," Gwen said with a long exhale. "When I stopped by, William was in a hurry for me to get back on the road."

"Do you think it was because she may have a clue about his dealings with other women? Or do you think that he was trying to cover up something about Bianca's murder?"

She nibbled at her lip. "I'm not the cop here, but my gut's telling me he didn't have anything to do with Bianca's murder. I don't think he was the one in your family's barn. He's not the kind of guy who would get his hands dirty. At least not like that. As for Monica, I don't think he does anything in front of her. Before the thing with Bianca, she and I used to be friends. She never whispered a word about him or his affairs to me."

"Did you know he was having affairs back then?"

"Honestly, I didn't know him that well. I just saw him between the normal comings and goings of things. I never liked him. He always treated Monica like she was an employee rather than his wife."

"What do you mean?"

She shrugged. "Once when I was waiting for her to finish getting ready, he came in and told her that he needed a new printer for his home office. Instead of recognizing that we had plans, he made us go pick out a new one and bring it back and set it up for him. He wasn't that busy. He could have done it himself, but no. It's just stupid little things like that. Like his life is so much more important than hers. It made me sick every time I was around them."

"Well, it's no wonder he cheats on her. He doesn't appreciate her."

"Just shoot me if you ever see me in a relationship like that," she said flippantly, then as though she realized that she was talking to him about a relationship, her face turned red and she started to stammer. "I mean… I don't want… You know. I just don't want to be with a man who treats me like that."

There were so many endearing things about her. No matter what happened between them, he could still like her for the person she had once been, and the wonderful, albeit confusing, woman she had become.

"What do you want, Gwen?" he asked, unable to help himself or the desire that started to fill him as she stammered over her words like she had when they were young. Yet, as he asked the question, he wasn't entirely sure he wanted to know the answer.

She bit at the side of her cheek as their eyes met. What was she trying to tell him with that look?

"I...I don't know, Wyatt," she said, her voice soft. "But I don't think crazy is a good look on me." She motioned toward the world outside the library. "I mean, like what happened at your place. I'm sorry. I don't know what happened back there, but I can't...I don't know. I guess I just want to be able to just *be* with you...or someone. I don't want to have to worry about other girls calling them. Or their wives. Or if they mean what they say. I'm just no good at the dating thing—I've been burned so much in the past. I mean, my ex was engaged *two months* after we broke up. I don't have it in me to play games again. It doesn't bring out the best in me. I'm so sorry."

"You did let a little bit of your crazy show," he said, with what he hoped was a comforting and dismissive laugh. "The good news is that I always liked your kind of crazy."

She tilted her head and gave him a smile that made his heart shift in his chest. "You say that, but I doubt you mean it. I'm a lot of work. And I'm a hard woman to date."

Was that her way of saying she would date him?

Is that what he wanted?

He liked her. He always had. And as understanding as he could be about what had happened back in his bathroom, he hadn't really thought she was open to anything. It was amazing how she continued to surprise him.

"And I'm probably even harder," he said in an attempt to be real. "I'm not around a lot. I'm always working, either at the department or helping out on the ranch. I don't know if I could make you happy, Gwen. I mean…I already tried once. Sure, we were young, but that doesn't change the fact that we failed." He stepped back from her, and for the first time he noticed how hot the room was. "You were right about what you said back at my place. Maybe it's not a good idea to go driving back down a dead-end road… We both know how it's gonna end. And, as much as you don't want your heart broken, I don't want mine to be torn to pieces either. Not again."

"I'm so sorry it has to be this way, Wyatt."

Her face fell and she stared down at the floor as she scuffed her shoe over the rough concrete.

"It's okay. I guess it's good that we're on the same page, at least." Even if he wasn't sure it was the page he wanted them to be on, he had to protect himself and her from being hurt again.

He took her by the hand. Her fingers were stiff and unyielding in his, and though he should have let her go, he couldn't force his body to do as his mind told. He thought about all the things he wanted to tell her—that he wanted her back in his life, that he didn't want to get hurt and that the thing he feared the most was falling in love.

He led her up the stairs and past the librarian.

"Thanks for everything," he said, giving the librarian a warm smile and a tip of his head.

She gave him a sour look, surely noticing him holding Gwen's hand, but he didn't care. Not waiting for her to answer, they walked through the front door.

As they stepped out onto the sidewalk he turned back to Gwen, unable to handle the tense silence between them any longer. "Let's just get through this. Then we can talk about things when I get back from Alaska."

She pulled her hand from his and frowned. "What are you talking about, *when you get back from Alaska*?"

Had he forgotten to tell her?

He stopped and turned toward her in an effort to deflect some of the blow. "Yeah…I have a prisoner transfer in a couple of days. I have to go up there, then bring him back to the county for his trial."

"When were you going to tell me that you were just going to leave me high and dry with Bianca's case? You just yelled at me about keeping secrets, yet here you are not telling me something like that. Don't you think I deserved to know you were going to push me and the case on someone else?" Her words came hard and fast, and each was like a fist.

"You have it all wrong, Gwen. I wasn't keeping anything from you. It just slipped my mind."

"Don't tell me that."

"No, really," he said, raising his hands in surrender. "I've had other things on my mind besides going." He gave her a soft grin; the grin he knew she loved.

She sighed, taking a second to collect herself. "So, you're not going to go on the trip?"

He grimaced. "That's not possible. Everything's set up for me to go. I have to. It's my job, Gwen."

As he looked at her, he couldn't help the feeling that he had been right. He was never going to be the kind of guy who could make her happy. There were just so many things standing in their way.

Even knowing that, he couldn't help the desire that filled him every time he looked into her lake-blue eyes. The wind kicked up and blew her scent toward him. He drew the aroma of flowers and sweet grass deep into his lungs. Why did everything have to be so alluring when it came to her? Everything but the torture they seemed to always inflict upon each other.

Gwen started walking down the sidewalk. Was she just going to leave him and walk back to the ranch? Was she that mad?

"What are you doing, Gwen? I'm sorry," he called out, catching up to her. "I didn't mean to hurt your feelings. It's just that there are just some things I can't change. My job is one of them."

Gwen turned on her heel. "I don't care

about your damn job, Wyatt. I get it. I was stupid to let what happened happen this morning. If anyone is sorry here, it's me."

How could he tell her that, even now when they were fighting, he wanted to be with her? That some feelings never went away?

"Wait, Gwen," he said, reaching for her hand, but she jerked away.

"Don't. No. Let's not put ourselves through this. Let's just get to the bottom of the case and each of us can go back to our own lives. We don't need to talk about it. We don't need to bring up old hurts—or new ones. Let's just let each other be. We're no good together."

He couldn't disagree with her more. Things weren't easy between them. There was too much history for things to be simple. But what they didn't have in ease, they made up for in passion. If they could just let go of some things, they could be like they were in the shower—laughing and truly letting each other see who they were at their core.

He loved her for the woman she was inside—if she would ever let him see that person again.

She started walking, making her way past the Pretties and Pastries café, and he trailed behind, unsure of how to proceed. No matter how he felt, he couldn't make her feel something too. And he'd already apologized for making the mistake of not telling her about Alaska. What more could she want?

Gwen stopped in front of Secret Secondhand. He glanced in the window. Monica was talking to a customer, but, as she noticed them, her face pinched and she gave a tight wave. Just as Frannie had told them, Monica had a large fresh bruise on her left eye. She turned away, covering her face in shadows.

Whatever had happened after Gwen had left had been something that Monica obviously wouldn't want to talk about. Had William hit her? Wyatt wanted to walk in and ask her about it, but from her body language, it was clear that she didn't want to see them.

All of his deputy spidey senses tingled. William was guilty of something. And, if Wyatt had to bet, William had something to do with Bianca's death. If Wyatt had learned one thing, it was that the type of men who used violence to control were often the same ones who ended up becoming murderers. Usually it wasn't intentional. Or at least that was what they loved to say in court—that they didn't mean to, or that things had just gotten out of hand.

He hated that kind of man—the kind who thought hitting was okay. No woman—heck, *no one*—deserved to live in a constant fear of physical violence. PFMA, partner or family member assault, were among his least favorite calls to take, and one of the most common. It seemed like most days he had at least one, if not two, calls in which he had to break up a family's fight.

Unfortunately, in the case of abuse, the woman was very unlikely to go against the husband. In the state of Montana, the court systems were starting to toe a harder line against perpetrators of domestic violence, but there still wasn't much they could do to protect the victims. There were hundreds of cases in which a woman finally got the strength, or hit rock bottom, and turned in the abuser— only to have the abuser get out of jail and murder the woman they felt was responsible for putting them behind bars.

It was a no-win system.

Gwen pulled on his hand. "Are we going in or what?"

He motioned toward Monica. "She didn't call the police and report anything. I bet you a hundred bucks that William hit her, but if you asked her what happened she'll have some stupid excuse—she ran into something, fell down the stairs…something."

"I know Monica. She'll open up to me."

"You said she hasn't in the past. Why do you think it would be different with me, a deputy, at your side?" He gave a cynical laugh. "The more you hang out with me, the more you'll see that this uniform tends to make everyone tighten up. We aren't going to get anywhere with Monica. I think it's better if we look into other things first. Namely, William. He's a hell of a good place to start as far as our list of suspects."

"Sure. If you think it's best, but…" She turned away from the window, but glanced back at Monica as if she was thinking about exactly how good their friendship was…and if what he was saying was true.

"Trust me about Monica. Before we can go to her, we need to figure out what motivates her. And what it will take to make her flip against her husband—that is, *if* her husband is the murderer. He may be nothing more than a piece of—"

"Oh, I can guarantee he's *that*," Gwen said, finishing his thought. "So, if we're not going to talk to Monica, what did you have in mind for your next step?"

He started walking back to the car, Gwen following. In truth, he didn't have much to go on, so he went with the first thing that came to mind. "The medical examiner was talking about Beuthanasia, but what I've been wondering is where it came from. Did she have it with her? Or did someone else have it? Does she have a partner in her vet practice? Or does she have an employee who would have access to the drug and had a problem with her?"

Gwen tapped on her lip. "There's always something going on at the clinic. You know, small-town stuff. But there's not been anything going on recently, at least nothing that she'd mentioned to me."

"Let's head over there." He glanced down at his watch. "They have to be up and running. Maybe we can talk to someone who has been working closely with Bianca—maybe they can tell us a little more about her affair with William."

He was grasping for straws, but that was exactly what an investigation normally was—following tiny leads, most that led nowhere… But once in a while, in a moment of intuition, of following that little wiggle in his gut, they led him to the answers he needed.

SHE WAS ACTING like a lunatic and she knew it. She wanted him, all of him, but the fear of being close to someone was nearly overwhelming. She had so much on her hands with her mother, her sister and the needs of the ranch. That, mixed with all the apprehension she was feeling… It was all so confusing.

All she could do was move through this one moment at a time, then one day, then one week. If he was the man she thought he was, he would understand and forgive her for the way she was feeling.

She glanced over at Wyatt. He turned toward Bianca's vet clinic. His caramel-colored eyes were hidden behind his aviators and he seemed focused on the road—maybe a little too focused. Was he avoiding talking to her? Was he trying to stop them from having another disagreement? Or was he just waiting for her to say something?

"How long are you going to be in Alaska?" she asked, hoping he was just waiting.

He sucked in a long breath that told her she may have been wrong.

"I know you have to go," she said, trying to take the edge off her question. "I know what your job entails. I guess I want to know more about the man you are—as my friend. That's all."

"As your *friend*?" He gave her a look she wasn't able to read—but the best she could guess was that it was halfway between questioning and confused.

"Yeah. The truth is, Wyatt, I've missed you." She sighed. "You were my whole life for so long. It was hard when I…I ended things. You helped me through so much, with my dad and all…and my mom. When you weren't around, it was like I had lost myself and who I was. I was a ghost of the person I had been. I lost everything. I never want to feel that way again."

"You couldn't, Gwen. You know who you are now. Who knows? Maybe it wasn't a bad thing that we broke up… You got to know who you are and I got to know who I am. We each got to go out in the world and experience things we wouldn't have if we'd stayed together."

She wasn't sure she agreed with him. If they'd stayed together, maybe they would have simply experienced the world together instead of apart—and maybe they both would have been better for it. Or maybe they both would have been so pulled to this town they would never have left. That had certainly been the case for her, and without a doubt, if she would have allowed their relationship to continue, he would have given up the world for her.

Now, rightly, he wouldn't even give up a trip to Alaska. Not that she blamed him, or didn't understand that he had to go. Plus, they'd only been speaking again for a couple of days. She couldn't expect anything from him.

She sighed. *Stop.* She had to stop. She couldn't pick apart everything he said, every choice he made and every feeling she had—it wasn't healthy. For either of them. For once, she just needed to go with the moment and let life happen. She couldn't micromanage this. She couldn't plan the unexpected.

Then again, some questions needed answering. "So you're not mad at me for the past? For breaking things off?"

His fingers gripped the steering wheel tight, but after a moment they loosened and he glanced over at her. "At first, I was like you—you were the only thing I knew. I loved you with all my heart. I didn't understand why you did what you did. I still don't. For being so young, we really were good together."

"We were." She nodded.

"Do you remember the barn?" he asked with a light laugh.

She thought back to the dozens of nights they had found themselves meeting up in his family's main barn at Dunrovin. They would sneak up into the hayloft and make out. He never pressured her for more, even though she had known exactly how badly she left him aching.

Her gentleman.

"What about the barn?" she asked with a wiggle of her brow.

He chuckled, and the sound made some of the heaviness in her disappear.

Yes, she just needed to let things be. What would happen would happen and she would have to accept their connection for what it was, not what she wanted it to be. If she didn't, she would be lucky if they even ended this investigation as friends.

Wyatt shifted slightly in the seat. "You remember the night we carved our initials in the post?"

She smiled. "That was the night of the Sadie Hawkins dance, right?"

He nodded. "Bianca went with us. Wasn't that when she was going after Rainier?"

She laughed as she thought back to the days when she and her sister had dreamed of marrying the brothers. "How life changes…"

"It was too bad they didn't work out."

Those had been the days before her father's death. The days they had still been innocent and untouched by tragedy. The days when her mother had still been functional.

"But she and Rainier…" he continued. "If you want to talk about two people who were completely different."

She laughed at the thought of her preppy sister dating their county's infamous bad boy. As soon as her parents had found out about their relationship, her father had put an end to it.

"Their relationship had some fireworks."

His eyebrow quirked as he looked over at her and smiled. "You mean like ours as of late?"

"I wouldn't consider this a relationship." She gave him a coy glance.

Wait. Did *he*?

"True, but…seeing you in that towel… You definitely brought out the animal in me."

She tried to restrain her grin. "Really?"

His smile widened. "I haven't been that

turned on in a long time. You have no idea what you do to me."

She reached over and sat her hand between them under the police-issued computer on the console. He let go of the steering wheel and slipped his fingers between hers.

They weren't anything beyond friends, but within her there was a glimmer of hope. Regardless of what she did to him, he had no idea what he did to her—or her heart.

Chapter Nine

The clinic was locked and someone had taped a closed sign to the door in between two plastic Santa decals. Wyatt was surprised at the lack of activity. He would have thought that, even with Bianca's death, the show would have needed to go on at her clinic. Animals always needed tending and phones would always ring. Yet the place was eerily quiet.

"Is this how the place normally is?" Wyatt asked as Gwen stopped beside him.

She shook her head. "No, but with everything that's been happening…someone must have let the employees know they weren't to come in." She walked around the side of the building toward the barn that normally housed the large animals that her sister couldn't see in the small clinic. "Even the barn's empty. That's strange."

"She had been working, right?"

Gwen shrugged. "As far as I know, but lately Bianca had been off. And the more and more I see, I guess I can understand why."

"You think it's possible someone just came in and cleared out the animals after they found out what happened?"

"For sure, but I don't know where they would have taken the animals that were in more serious condition. But maybe she didn't have any super serious cases or something."

Wyatt nodded. There was something wrong about the place. If some well-meaning person had taken the animals, he would have thought they would have left a note or something, but there was nothing besides the sign on the front door to let anyone know what was going on.

"I think you should wait in the car," he said, motioning toward his patrol unit. "Let me clear the building, then I'll come get you."

"There's no way I'm going to let you go in there alone. Besides, there's nothing to worry about." She peered in the front picture window with her hand over her eyes in an attempt to shield the evening sun from her eyes.

"Anything?" he asked as she turned back to him.

"I can't see." She shook her head. "Hold

on," she said, reaching down into her pocket and drawing out a key ring that was chock-full of a variety of brass and aluminum keys. "I think she gave me a key in case I ever needed it. I don't think this is what she had in mind at the time, but..." She flipped through the keys and stopped at a brass one the same color as the doorknob.

She slipped the key into the lock and clicked it open. The door opened with a long, shrill squeak. For a moment, Gwen stood there just staring. Wyatt moved closer to her, trying to see what she was looking at.

"Holy..." he said, looking in.

There was dog food strewn across the floor, and all the papers that normally sat on the counter were thrown around the room. Every picture was crooked or had been taken off the wall and tossed on the floor. The receptionist's computer screen was cracked and the keyboard was hanging over the edge of the desk by its cord—it made the shrill tone of a phone that had been off the hook for too long. Even the waiting room chairs were overturned and pulled away from the walls.

Whoever had come into this place wasn't there just to steal; they had been there to destroy. They must have hated Bianca and her work. Was it possible that whoever was behind this had been a jilted customer or someone who had felt that she had done them wrong?

Monica came to his mind. Could she have found out about Bianca's affair with William? Perhaps she went to Bianca's cabin, then here to take her down? Maybe when she didn't find Bianca she had gone to the ranch. Or maybe she had come here first and had stolen the Beuthanasia and then gone to Bianca's cabin.

Gwen walked toward the back of the clinic, pushing past the half door that led to the back.

"Don't touch anything," he called. "I want to get my team in. Maybe they can pull some prints."

Gwen stopped and turned around. "Oh, I'm sure they can pull hundreds of prints. There are normally at least a hundred people in and out of this building in a single working day. You could probably pull most of the people's prints from this town—everyone comes to my sister for their livestock."

Whoever had done this had put thought behind what they wanted to do and how they wanted to do it. This was a crime of anger and perhaps revenge, but it wasn't one done carelessly.

Regardless, he had to get his people in here

and give it a shot. He couldn't call the game until it had been played.

"Don't go back there alone, Gwen," he said, motioning for her to stay put. "I need to clear the place before we go poking around. We don't want to surprise anyone if they are still here."

Even as he spoke, he knew he was being overly protective. It was unlikely anyone else was in the building, but he had to keep Gwen safe and, if they got their hands on the perpetrator, he would have to have all his ducks in a row for the prosecuting attorney. He wouldn't be able to look himself in the mirror if whoever was behind all this got to walk on a technicality—something every defense attorney loved.

He moved after her down the hall and took the lead. The front had been a mess, but the back of the clinic was even worse. Every cupboard was opened and a medley of supplies from gauze to bottles of Betadine were torn off the shelves and scattered through the hallways and rooms. There was a room filled with cages, for what he assumed was for the small animals that came through the clinic, but the pens were empty and half of them stood open.

Bianca's office sat next to that small room.

Every drawer of her black metal desk was open and the one on the right bottom sat crooked, like someone had pulled on it just a little too hard. Broken glass littered the top of her desk and an empty, bent frame was thrown on top of her nameplate.

"Do you know what picture she had on her desk?" he asked, pointing toward the frame.

"Sure, that was one from this year's Fourth of July. We had a big barbecue at the ranch. Everyone was there and we got a photo. It was one of the best parties we've ever had."

"Could you name some of the people from the picture?"

She tapped on her lip and looked toward the ceiling like she could pull the faces out of the air. "Well… We were there, Mom, Bianca and me. Then there were some people from around town—a lot of my mom's friends from the bar. There was the staff from here. And your brother's ex-wife, Alli, with her sister, Christina, and Winnie. Just about everyone we knew came." Her mouth went into an O shape. "And the Poes were there… William and Monica."

"Were they in the picture?"

She nodded. "I'm sure."

He sighed. Everything came back to the

Poes. There was no question they were involved in this, but it was up to him to figure out exactly how deep their connections lay.

"Did everyone at the party get a picture? Or did your sister post it to Facebook or anything?"

"I don't think so. And Bianca doesn't do the whole social media thing."

He didn't either. And to be honest, he didn't mind it. Many of the PFMAs he was called on seemed to involve one or more of the social media sites. It was a testament to the times that so many feelings could be hurt with just a few mistyped words or an inferred slight that originated on a screen.

Was it possible that this case had something to do with a slight? Maybe someone besides Monica had found out about William and Bianca's affair and had grown jealous.

It seemed like a stretch. Monica and William seemed like the most likely suspects. In cases like these, most often the wife had found out and and had come after the girlfriend. And usually deaths perpetrated by women were just like Bianca's—passive kills—murders that involved a poison or some kind of implement that wasn't as brutal, and one where the killer didn't have to actually watch the person die.

The signs were beginning to point more and more in the direction of a woman as the killer, but that didn't take William off the suspect list. He was just the kind of guy who would also commit a passive murder. He didn't want to get his hands dirty, but maybe he would if the conditions were right—like if Bianca was blackmailing him.

There were still so many missing elements keeping Wyatt from fully understanding this case, but as he walked out of Bianca's office, for the first time since they started, he knew he was getting closer to pinning the perpetrator down.

In the back of the clinic there was a refrigerator. Its door was ajar, and medications had spilled out of it. He moved closer. In the open cupboard next to the fridge, there was a lockbox.

"Is this where your sister would have kept the scheduled medications?" he asked, pointing toward the box.

"What's that?" Gwen asked, stopping beside him.

"Those are the drugs that the DEA deems

dangerous and addictive if not used properly—you know, like the Beuthanasia."

"Oh, you mean is that where she keeps— er, *kept*—her narcs?" she asked.

"Not all scheduled meds are narcs, but yeah. Is that where she kept them?"

Gwen nodded. "I think so. Why?"

He knelt down by the box. "It's still locked, which means one of two things. Either the perp took the drugs from the cabinet while it was still open, which means they wouldn't have had to turn the place over. Or, what I believe, is that they took the drugs from Bianca's bag at Dunrovin. But if I'm right, we're going to have to prove it."

"Let's say you're right. Let's say they took the drugs from her bag in the barn. What does that change?"

He smiled as he felt another piece of his investigation fall into place. "If they didn't take the drugs while they were here, maybe it means they weren't really planning on killing her. Maybe they were following her, watching her work. When she went to see the mare, a mare that she may have been prepared to put to sleep, the perp saw an opportunity to make the kill—and they took it."

"I'm not following," Gwen said with a frown.

"If they hadn't been planning to kill her, maybe they were a little less prepared. Maybe they made a mistake in their haste. Maybe they forgot to wear gloves when they went through her bag. And Bianca was probably the only other one to touch it, which means maybe we can get the prints we need."

Gwen sucked in a breath.

"We need to find your sister's vet bag."

"Alli said your mother had been in the barn after your team had been through. Maybe she found it somewhere, or can at least tell us whether or not she saw it."

He pulled his phone out of his pocket and dialed his mom. He walked back to his car, took out the camera he kept in the trunk and made his way back into the building.

His mom answered on the second ring. "How's it going, sweetie?"

No matter how old he got, his foster mother would always call him "sweetie," and as much as it probably would have bothered other men, it was one of the many things he loved about her. She was the kind who always put everyone else ahead of herself, sometimes to a fault. She had a habit of bringing on employees who had dark pasts—pasts that usually came back to bite her in the butt.

Once, Eloise Fitzgerald had hired a felon—the man had worked in the guest quarters, cleaning and taking care of the rooms. Two weeks after he'd been brought on, he'd broken into one of the rooms, stolen the guest's keys and made off with their car. The ranch's insurance had taken a hit, and the car had later been found abandoned at the Canadian border. They didn't talk about it and she hadn't hired another known felon since, but she was still a sucker for sob stories.

"Good." He started to take pictures of the scene. "I was calling because Alli mentioned that you had been in the barn after Lyle and Steve went over the scene. By chance did you see Bianca's bag lying around anywhere? They didn't report finding a bag, but there should have been one on scene."

"Didn't you look when you were there?"

He hadn't come in until later, and when he'd arrived on scene it had been busy thanks to the coming and going of Lyle and Steve. It was only because he'd volunteered to notify the next of kin that he had even gotten the case. "I did, but Lyle and Steve took point."

"Lyle and Steve are lucky they found the barn. You do know that, right?" his mother said with a sharp laugh. "I mean those two men… How are they working at the same department as you? I can't believe you aren't just flying up the ranks over there."

She wasn't wrong about Steve and Lyle, but he couldn't control the only men who were his department's acting forensics team. The only things he could control were what he did with this case and how he could help the woman whose life it impacted the most.

"Mom, the bag. Did you see it?" he asked, trying to avoid falling into the chatting trap with his mother.

It had been a while since he'd seen or spoken to her, and no doubt she was chomping at the bit to hear about the case and how it was playing out. She was kind and smart, but she was also probably worrying about the impact the case would have on her business—not that she would bring it up to him.

"What did the bag look like?" she asked in a way that he couldn't decide if she was being coy or if she really had no idea what he was talking about.

"Don't play, Mom. You know. It's black. Kind of like a doctor's bag. Likely full of vet supplies." He looked over at Gwen, who was mimicking the shape with her hands.

"Oh, that?" his mom said. "I assumed you

all must have been done with it, so I dropped it off at the Widow Maker a couple of hours ago."

"Widow Maker?" He thought of Carla and her penchant for tossing raw eggs. He could only imagine how she would treat his mother—a woman Carla hadn't spoken to since the day of her husband's funeral. "*You* went to the Widow Maker? Why didn't you just leave it for me?"

Gwen's mouth opened with surprise. "She did what?"

There was a slight pause on the other end of the phone. "Sometimes the most honorable thing isn't the easiest, Wyatt."

It was a lesson his mother had drilled into him a long time ago, but he never grew above hearing it.

"This isn't about being honorable, Mom—"

"Besides, Carla was quite nice," his mother continued, cutting him off. "She even invited me in for a cup of joe. I think she's very lonely and hurt with Bianca's death and... Well, *you know.*"

She didn't have to remind him of their battered pasts.

"Are you sure she didn't invite you in so

she could poison your coffee? Or was she drunk again?"

"She's still a drunk?" his mother asked.

He glanced over at Gwen. She was shaking her head as she pinched the bridge of her nose. "It doesn't matter. Did you go in the house?"

"I chatted with her a bit on the porch, but there was work that needed tending to at the ranch. With that mare down and everything up in the air with...*things*, well, I just didn't feel good being gone for too long. She seemed to understand. But it might be nice if you stopped by and visited with her for a bit. She wanted to talk about you."

The woman who had pelted his patrol unit yesterday wanted to talk about him? Either she was slobbering drunk, or she had sobered up and forgotten her earlier egg warfare and the gun she'd pulled on him.

He sighed. The last thing he wanted to do was have another run-in with that woman, but if she had the bag, her place was his next stop.

He dropped his hand down on the counter and papers slipped to the floor. It was about right. This day had seemed not only to have started with manure, but was seemingly destined to end with it as well.

Gwen ran her hands through her blond

hair, and it caught the light that was streaming through the windows of the back room.

What he would give to be back in the shower and escaping from reality.

Chapter Ten

As she trudged up to the front door of the ranch house and kicked the snow off her boots, Gwen couldn't help but feel like she was headed to the gallows. After her mother's scene in the driveway and the Taser, regardless of the show she had put on for Eloise Fitzgerald, this wasn't going to go well.

The door was unlocked, but before she stepped inside, she turned back to Wyatt.

His eyes were stormy. No matter how much she felt like she was going to the gallows, he was the one who *looked* it. His shoulders were rounded and his hands were opening and closing into tight fists as he stared in the front window.

The living room's curtains were drawn shut, blocking the last of the evening light from seeping through and illuminating the mess that was their lives.

She hated this place. Every time she came to the door it felt like she was entering her own personal hell. It was a reaction that had been learned over years of coming to this door and not knowing what she would find inside.

Once, when she'd been about twenty, she'd come home to find her mother smearing peanut butter on herself. She had tried to have her mother see a therapist afterward, but her mother had sworn the incident was because she had been cleaning up a downed pine and needed to get the sap off her skin. It was a story she could have bought had her mother not been buck naked. And drunk.

She glanced back to the man on death row. He stared at the door as he sucked in a long breath.

"Are you sure that you want to go inside? I can just run in, get the bag and get out. You don't have to put yourself through this," she said, motioning toward the chipped door.

Wyatt shook his head. "It's fine," he said, but there was a hardness to his voice she hadn't heard him use before.

Was that his officer voice? If it was, she could see why he was good at his job. He could probably scare the wits out of any criminal if he came at them with that kind of edge during an arrest or interrogation. As it was, the sound made her core tighten and a strange, unwelcome surge of apprehension moved through her. This wasn't a good idea. She should have just called her mother.

But it was too late to turn back now.

Hopefully her mother wasn't even home. She looked down at her watch. It was more than possible that Carla would be at the bar by now. And if she was, all the unpleasantness could be avoided. And heck, maybe if things continued on between her and Wyatt in the same way—with their constant failure to find a balance between their past, present and future—well, maybe he would never have to see her mother again.

The thought of them not working out coated her in a layer of heavy sadness.

Whatever they were or had been, it didn't really matter. What mattered was the longing she had felt when she'd been standing outside his trailer and the thrill when she'd been in his arms.

She pushed open the door and walked in ahead of Wyatt. Every part of her begged that her mother would be anywhere but here. Yet as she walked into the living room, she heard the familiar banging of the cabinets as her mother moved around in the kitchen.

Sometimes it was like she had no luck at all.

She looked over at Wyatt, and even in the near darkness of the room she could still see flashes of the tempest in his eyes.

"Why don't you wait here? I'll go in and find out where she put the bag. No need to start a *thing*." She held up her hand, checking him as though he was some kind of animal that she could control.

She should have known better.

"Gwen, I'm not letting you walk back there alone. What if whoever is behind your sister's death broke into your house? What if it's not your mother in there? Or what if she's being held captive?" He motioned to the door that led to the farm-style kitchen. "I'm not letting you walk into trouble."

"I hate to mention this, but…" She gave a nervous laugh. "Regardless of who's standing in that kitchen, there's going to be some amount of fireworks."

He motioned her forward, not taking her polite no as an answer. Sometimes he was so pushy and controlling, but at the same time his concern for her safety made him all that much more lovable.

"You know I'm looking forward to seeing your mother about as much as I'd look forward to getting a root canal. Actually, I'd take the root canal."

She chuckled. "Mom, you in there?" she called, afraid to let her thoughts go any further.

There was an unintelligible grumble from her mother inside the kitchen.

"Seriously," she said, motioning to Wyatt. "Wait for a minute. Let me make sure she's at least wearing clothing. If anything goes wrong, or if you are concerned in any way, you are welcome to come in. But you know my mother. I have no idea what kind of state she's going to be in."

Wyatt nodded. "Okay, but if I think anything's going haywire, I'm coming in."

Before she had time to think about what she was doing, she leaned in and gave him a quick peck on his stubbled cheek. Wyatt looked at her with wide eyes and she smiled. He was such a good man.

"Thanks." She turned and entered the kitchen, ignoring the desire she had to turn and tell Wyatt exactly what she thought of him—and how sorry she was for their mis-understanding back at his place.

How differently the day would have gone if she hadn't let her stupid emotions and in-securities get in the way.

In the kitchen, her mother was standing by the fridge. Her face was a shade of red Gwen recognized from her mother's many nights of drinking.

"How much have you had?"

Her mother looked up. There was a glass of vodka in her hand and, as she noticed Gwen looking, she pushed it behind her back like she was a kid caught in some guilty act.

"I don't know whatcher talking about," Carla said, her words slurred with drunken-ness. But as she spoke she forgot about hid-ing the drink in her hand and brought it back around where Gwen could see it.

Gwen gave a resigned sigh. "Mrs. Fitzger-ald said she stopped by here today and talked to you. Is that right?"

Her mother took a long drink, her need to hide outweighed by her desire for more. "I played all nicey-nicey, but she's still a piece of work. She thinks she's all high and mighty. Like her life don't stink…" She took another drink.

"Did she drop anything off?" Gwen couldn't help but feel like she was talking to a two-year-old.

Her mother shrugged, but her gaze moved to the back door where Bianca's vet bag sat on the counter. Gwen moved toward it, but her mother stepped in her way.

"Are you shacking up with that boy Wyatt?"

Gwen looked back at the door, praying Wyatt couldn't hear their conversation. He didn't need to hear her mother's smear campaign or anything else she probably had to say right now.

"Do I need to remind you of what he done to me? He had no right to tase me." Her mother picked up the nearly empty bottle of vodka that sat on the kitchen table and re-filled her glass.

"You're lucky he didn't arrest you. He could have. And think about how badly you'd be detoxing if he had."

"He didn't have nothing on me. I'm gonna sue him and the county. They're gonna have a real mess on their hands."

The only mess here was her.

"I shoulda sued them all for more. Do you remember the pissy little settlement his family's insurance gave us?"

Her mother had made it a nearly daily habit of complaining about how they had only gotten forty thousand dollars from the Dunrovin's insurance company. That, added to her father's life insurance, had covered his burial and about six months of the ranch's overhead costs. Six months in which her mother had fallen deeper and deeper into her depression—a depression that seemed to never end thanks to the constant numb of alcohol.

Gwen walked over and pried the glass from her fingers. "Aren't you tired of acting like this? Of feeling this way? It's been long enough. And now with Bianca gone... This isn't going to help you or me get through this."

Her mother reached after her as she walked to the sink and poured the drink down the drain.

"No!" her mother called, running to the sink. She grabbed the glass out of Gwen's hand and swirled her finger around the rim. "Who do you think you are? That was mine. I paid for it. I pay for everything in this dang place. You got no right to come in here and take anything of mine—especially in a week like this."

"I'm the one who runs this ranch, Mother. Do I need to remind you how little you do?"

She knew now was a poor time to pick a fight, but she couldn't stand idly by and let her mother try to slowly kill her with the lashes lain by her words. Not anymore.

"How dare you, Gwyneth Marie Johansen." Her mother tried to take on an air of authority by using her full name, but it came out as a slow, slurry mess of syllables that made her sound even drunker than before.

Wyatt stepped into the kitchen. "Mrs. Johansen," he said, greeting her with a dip of the head. "I hope you're feeling better."

"What the hell are you doing here?" She motioned her glass toward Wyatt, then turned and lifted her shirt. There, on the side of her waist, was an angry black-and-blue mark where the Taser's prongs had bitten into her skin. "Look what you did to me, you bastard. I hope you feel real good about taking down an old woman. What else are you gonna do to me? Get Gwen killed—just like you did with Bianca and my husband? You want to kill my whole damned family. Admit it."

She staggered as she moved toward Wyatt. The glass slipped in her hand and fell to the floor, shattering. The shards of glass spewed across the linoleum, landing on the tips of Gwen's boots.

Her mother kept moving, seemingly unaware of the glass and the scene she was causing.

"Carla, don't move," Wyatt ordered, motioning at her mother's bare feet. "There's glass all over the floor. If you step, you're going to cut yourself up. Just stay where you are and we'll clean this up."

Her mother hiccupped, and she listed to the left so hard she was forced to grab the counter. The glass crunched under her and dots of blood oozed out from beneath the soles of her feet.

"Carla." Wyatt rushed to her side, wrapping his arm around her. "I told you to stay put. Are you okay?"

She tried to push his arms away, but the movement was feeble and weak. Normally her mother was so strong when she was drunk that she could nearly take down a full-grown moose.

"I…I got…this," her mother said, her words suddenly even more slurred and gummed together than before.

She fell into Wyatt's arms.

Something was very wrong.

"What…did ya do to me?" her mother asked, looking at Wyatt like he had slipped her a roofie.

"How much did you drink, Mrs. Johansen? Really. It's important you tell me."

Carla slipped down, forcing him to hold her as she gently slid to the floor and her body rested along the bits of glass. Her eyes started to close.

"Mrs. Johansen! Don't go to sleep. Stay awake." Wyatt reached down to his handset and, speaking in codes, called an ambulance. "Does your mother normally drink to this point?"

"She drinks a lot. You saw how she can be." Gwen motioned toward the driveway. "That's how she usually is. Sometimes she's so good at this that she can even seem sober. This isn't like her."

Her mother started to convulse and white foam poured from her lips. Wyatt rolled her over on her side and held her head so she wouldn't choke.

He looked up at Gwen and there was a look of panic in his eyes.

She dropped to her knees, taking her mother's hand. "Mom. Mom!" she called as Carla's eyes rolled back into her head so only the whites showed. "Stay with us! I'm so sorry... No... Mom, don't leave."

Chapter Eleven

The St. James Hospital emergency room was a flurry of motion as the doctor jogged past them toward Carla's room. The EMTs stood outside, watching as the nurses took her vitals and asked questions about the scene.

Wyatt wanted to be angry at Carla for what she had done, but he couldn't feel anything except a deep pooling sadness for Gwen. She had such a tough life. It was like bad luck was constantly flying right over her and just waiting for the next moment it could swoop in and scavenge away another piece of what she loved.

No wonder she was so resistant to moving their relationship into anything serious—or toward anything at all.

Then again, she had kissed his cheek back at her mother's place, before everything had hit the fan. That had to have meant something, didn't it? Or had it simply been her way of thanking him for trying to take care of her?

He wished she came with a set of written instructions, or maybe a procedure manual— anything that could help him make sense of all the emotions and questions that swirled through him.

He glanced over at her. There were dark circles under her eyes and her hair was disheveled. Reaching over, he smoothed her hair. She looked up at him and their eyes met, and he was reminded of how scared she had been when she had watched her mother have the seizure. No matter how much she must hate her mother sometimes, and regardless of how mad or embarrassed the woman made her, Carla would always be her mom.

He could understand that kind of forgiveness and love. He hated to think or talk about it, but his mind went back to the pool of blackness that was his past before he'd come to the Fitzgeralds. His mother, a drug addict, had sold herself in order to support her drug habit, until one day she was arrested.

She hadn't bothered to tell the police she'd left a child, him, at home. He had been five at the time; just old enough to remember the feeling of being all alone in the middle of the night, listening to the sounds that came with living in a cheap motel.

Some nights he could still remember the smell of her, the thick vanilla perfume mixed with the pungent odor of cigarettes.

He hated her now, but he could still remember on the day the police had come to take him away and he'd been placed into the foster care system, being scared and telling them how much he missed and loved his mommy.

Oh, those wounds that would never heal.

For some, those like him and Gwen, these were wounds they would carry with them for their entire lifetime.

He reached down and laced his fingers between hers. Perhaps together they could both heal, if only she would let them try.

"Do you think she's going to be okay?" Gwen asked, squeezing his fingers.

He nodded as he rubbed a small circle on the back of her hand with his thumb. "I think she'll be fine, really…"

Gwen lifted their entwined hands. "Do you know that I've always hated those little circles you make with your thumb? It used to drive me crazy when we were younger."

He stopped moving his thumb. "Oh," he

said, trying not to be embarrassed. "Why didn't you tell me? I would have stopped."

She pulled their hands to her face and brushed the back of his hand against her cheek. "Don't stop. I don't want you to stop."

Her face was soft and warm against his skin and he made a slow, meticulous circle over the back of her hand.

"Are you sure?" He wasn't quite sure if they were talking about the circles or something else.

"Sometimes what we think drives us crazy are the things we end up missing the most."

"I'm glad you missed me," he said with a small, playful smile.

Some of the darkness lifted from her eyes. "I missed you more than you can know. I'm so sorry, Wyatt. I just thought…"

He leaned in and kissed the back of her hand. As much as he wanted to hear what she had to say, he didn't want her to regret her decision when she was better rested and not under the stresses of the day.

"It's okay, Gwen. I know. And I'm sorry, too, but…"

She gave him a weak smile. "*But* is right. And for now, *but* is good enough."

Dr. Richards walked out of the hospital

room, toweling off his hands. He looked around the ER and, spotting them, he made his way over. "I've got good news."

Gwen shifted as though her knees were going to give out, and Wyatt wrapped his arm around her in an effort to keep her from falling.

"What is it? What happened?" Her words came in a flurry.

Dr. Richards motioned to the bank of chairs that sat against the far wall. "Do you wish to sit down?"

Gwen shook her head. She was usually so strong—sometimes almost to a fault. At least this time, she was just letting Wyatt support and comfort her.

Wyatt nodded for Dr. Richards to continue.

"While she isn't out of the woods, your mother should pull through this."

"What is *this*? What happened to her?" Gwen asked, her voice high with stress.

The doctor looked back toward the nurses' station and the stack of charts like he wanted to go grab one, but he stopped himself and turned back. "We received the results of the toxicology screen. It looks as though your mother may have overdosed on Tramadol."

"Tramadol?" Gwen repeated.

"Yes, it's a pain med. We prescribe it frequently. Do you know where your mother may have gotten the drug?"

She shook her head. "My mother hasn't seen a doctor in at least ten years. There's no way she could have had access to a medication like that."

There was a sick feeling in the pit of Wyatt's stomach. "Isn't Tramadol frequently used by veterinarians?"

Gwen jerked in his arms.

Dr. Richards nodded. "Sure, I think it's actually utilized quite often in their line of work."

"Is it something that could have been in your sister's bag?" Wyatt asked, looking at Gwen.

She was staring off into space as though she were struggling to understand everything that was happening around her. "Yeah...I know Bianca used it all the time. She kept it around for the dogs on the ranch."

"So your mother had some sort of access?"

"Sure," she said, looking at him. "But whatever she may do as far as drinking, she's never been suicidal. She too ornery to have done this to herself."

"You mean, before Bianca's death." Wyatt

squeezed her hand tighter. "Do you think she would have done it now?"

Gwen shook her head. "No. Think about it. She acted like she didn't know what was going on. If she had been trying to kill herself, don't you think she would have had more of a clue?"

"Do you think it's possible she was just trying to smooth off some of the rough edges, and somehow it got out of hand?" the doctor asked.

Gwen looked over at him. "My mother didn't take an ibuprofen. I'm not kidding. For her, alcohol could cure anything. She wasn't trying to commit suicide."

"Was anyone around her or at the house before the time of the incident?" Dr. Richards asked.

The sick feeling in Wyatt's stomach worsened and he glanced over at Gwen. "My mother…my mom was there. She's the one who dropped off the bag. But she'd never drug Carla. She didn't have a bad thing to say about your mom. Ever. Not even with everything that's happened between our families. She's a saint."

Gwen chewed on her lip as she continued to stare into space. "No. It couldn't have been her. But it had to have been someone who had access to the bag and my mother's booze."

Wyatt looked at his phone to check the status of the forensics team. He lifted it so she could see the email they'd sent him. "My team is just wrapping up at the vet clinic," he said, slipping the phone back into his pocket. "I'll have them stop by your mom's for the bag. Hopefully then we can figure out exactly what's going on."

Gwen nodded, but he could have sworn she hadn't blinked in at least a minute.

A thought struck him. It was possible that whoever had killed Bianca may have been trying to kill Carla as well. Maybe they were targeting the women of Widow Maker Ranch. If that was the case, it was only a matter of time until they came after Gwen.

"Please keep Carla under the close watch of hospital staff and security, okay?" Wyatt said with a nod to Dr. Richards. "And please let me know if Carla's condition takes a turn." He pointed to his phone. "I'll be available anytime."

"No problem. I'll be in contact," Dr. Richards said with a serious look. "I'll make her our unit's number one priority. She won't be left alone."

Wyatt turned to Gwen. "Now, let's get you home so you can get some much-needed rest."

She didn't bat an eye as she nodded.

He was still holding her, so instead of letting go, he pulled her up into his arms and carried her. She laid her head on his shoulder and looped her arms around his neck. He'd never felt anything better.

Tonight, he wouldn't leave her side. No matter what, he would be there to keep her safe.

THE PAIN IN Gwen's chest, the one that always seemed to be there, was suddenly all-consuming, and for the first time in her life, she realized it wasn't the pain of loss. No. It was the pain that came with living. Of being tired of the constant beating life gave her. Of being perpetually confused as she sorted through the feelings in her heart and the thoughts in her head. More than anything, it was the pain of being pulled between the dreams she had for her life and the reality of it.

Nothing was ever going to change. She would forever be taking care of her mother and the mess she had become.

She was crazy to hope for anything different. As much as she had begged for her mother to stay and fight for her life, in a deep, dark place in Gwen's heart she secretly wished her mother could have simply fallen to the floor and slipped away. And Gwen hated herself for it.

She looked out from under her eyelashes. Wyatt was asleep in the recliner beside his bed.

He had kept his promise to stay by her side for the night. He hadn't even acted like he wanted the bed, nor had she pushed it. Instead she had simply let him carry her in and lay her in the bed, clothing and all, and tuck her in as if she were a child—a child in desperate need of tenderness and care.

She stared at his sleeping face. It was a face she had looked at thousands of times over the years, but for once she felt like she was truly seeing him for the man he was. At times he was imperfect, but those imperfections—the need to protect at all costs, his stoicism, the fear he seemed to have about opening up—only made him seem hotter.

And admittedly, she couldn't blame him for his fear of opening up. She was part of the reason he felt the way he did. It was an injury that she would never forgive herself for. He hadn't deserved to have his dreams crushed by her—even if she had thought it had been for all the right reasons.

Beyond his endearingly beautiful imperfections there were so many other reasons to fall. She knew him. She could close her eyes and see his face in perfect detail. She knew his smile when he was truly, sublimely happy versus the smile he shared with the world. And she knew the sound he made when he slipped into the comfort of sleep.

Part of her wanted to reach out, to wake him up and pull him into her arms, to feel him around her and bask in his warmth. Yet seeing him there, resting peacefully, she didn't want to disturb him. He'd had just as hard a day as she had. And maybe that self-sacrifice and compromise was the real mark of true, undying love—even if it was a love she may never get to fully realize.

Chapter Twelve

Sometimes there just wasn't enough coffee in the world. Wyatt felt like he had been hit by a Mack truck. Wyatt's neck ached after the night sleeping in the chair, but it was worth it—especially when he'd come in after morning chores and sat and watched as Gwen opened her eyes to the morning light.

She was so beautiful. He could have sat there all day, watching her breathe as the sun cascaded in through the curtains, flooding the sweet lines of her face. She had always been his dream. All of her. Yet some dreams just weren't meant to be realized.

Or maybe it was some cosmic joke, and he was still in the middle of learning something he hadn't quite yet grasped.

He pulled a long drink from his steaming cup and set it back in the car's cup holder.

"You okay?" Gwen asked as she clicked her seat belt into place. "Are you sure you want to run to the neighbor's? We can wait a bit."

"No, I'm fine. I already fed the horses, and it's just the west pasture with the cattle, right?"

She nodded. "You fed them all? Wow, I'm impressed. Thanks."

"You're welcome. Thought you needed to sleep in."

"I thought it was my turn," she teased, with a wink.

He laughed. "By the way," he continued, "I talked to the doctor this morning. Your mom's doing well. They're going to keep her for a bit, monitor her vitals until they're sure she's out of the woods with this. They're worried, however, that she'll start going through detox if they keep her too long."

The smile on her face disappeared, and he wished he hadn't brought up her mother. It was always one topic that he should avoid, but with things being what they were it was nearly impossible. Yet he would have done anything to bring the smile back to her lips.

"Did they ask her if she took the pills?" Gwen sighed.

"She didn't remember anything. And she

said she couldn't remember where she had gotten the vodka. She made it sound like you had left it for her."

"I never buy her alcohol. She's full of crap." Gwen sighed and she looked out the window as he started the car. "She's trying to stir the pot and make it sound like I enable her. I hope you told the doctor what kind of woman my mother can be."

"I didn't have that kind of time, but I happen to know that Dr. Richards knows a person can't be weighed and measured by their kin."

"Well, at least that's something." Gwen laughed. "Did he learn anything about her mental state? You know, whether or not he thought she could have wanted to end things?"

"From what he said, he didn't think she had made any conscious choice. They aren't going to seek psych for her."

"I don't think it would be a bad thing. She needs help. Maybe this can be her rock bottom."

He hated to tell her, but most rock bottoms—the moment when an addict decides to turn their life around—were myths. It took near death to make an addict realize they had a problem, and sometimes even that wouldn't work—and death was the only way to end their addiction.

For his biological mother, prostitution and jail were the norm, not the exception. And, in the case of Carla, she was probably just as desensitized as his mother had been. It was probably not the first time she found herself on the floor after a day spent drinking—for her, it was probably just another day she didn't remember.

He glanced over at Gwen. Her mother needed help to step out of her addiction, but if she did seek rehabilitation, Gwen would have to remodel her life into something completely new and foreign—it would be a life for just her—and he couldn't have been happier for her and the idea of her freedom.

He took another drink of his coffee and started down the road to the neighbor's house. The caffeine was kicking in. Maybe there was hope for the day after all.

They bumped down the driveway toward the Widow Maker and a house that used to be part of the ranch, but had been sold off in order for the Johansen women to make ends meet. Now an older couple who had retired and moved to Montana from Chicago lived in it. The place was well kept. Fake bunches of red poinsettias filled the flower baskets on each side of the porch. As they parked and made their way to the door, a Border collie bounded around from the backyard to greet them.

"Hiya, pup," Wyatt said, squatting down to give the dog a good scratch behind the ears. He'd always loved animals.

"His name's Rufio. You know, like the boy from the movie *Hook*." A woman in her mid-fifties stepped out from the side of the house from which the dog had come.

"Great movie," Wyatt said. "I loved watching it when I was a kid." He gave a slight wave in greeting as the woman stepped up onto the porch. "Name's Deputy Fitzgerald. I was just hoping I could ask you a few questions if you wouldn't mind."

"Oh, I know who you are. Who wouldn't in this town? I'm Dorothy Donaldson," the woman said with a knowing smile. "Your mother and I play cribbage down at the Fraternal Order of Eagles clubhouse about every other Saturday. She tells me all about you and your brothers. She's proud of you boys."

The thought of his mother expounding on him to strangers made him uncomfortable. "I don't know what she could've told you about. I just get up and go to work every morning."

"That's a heck of a lot more than what some kids do these days." Dorothy rubbed her gloved hands together and sent bits of snow to the ground. She glanced over at Gwen. "And how are you doing today? It's nice to see you. How's your mother doing?"

Gwen gave a polite smile, the one that masked all the pain she was feeling inside— he knew it all too well. "Actually we're here about her."

"Is that right?" Dorothy said, looking at Wyatt. "What can I help you with? Has she gone missing?"

He thought back to the moment he had first seen Gwen again, before he'd told her about Bianca's death, to the reaction she'd had at seeing him on their doorstep. She had been so angry with her mother for some mistake she had assumed she'd made, but now it made more sense. It seemed as though Carla had a bigger reputation as the town mischief maker than he had realized.

"Not missing," Gwen continued. "Not this time. Actually, she was drugged last night."

Wyatt nodded. "And we were wondering if

you, by chance, happened to see anyone coming or going yesterday?"

"Well, there was your mother, Wyatt." Dorothy motioned toward the road. "She stopped by here on her way over. She said she had to drop something off."

"Did you see anybody else?"

The woman puckered her lips as she thought, and the action made him wonder if she was a recovering smoker.

"After your mother left... I think there was another car. I couldn't tell you the model."

"But it was a car? Not a truck or an SUV?" Wyatt asked, pressing her to get the best description he could get.

"No, it was definitely a car. Not one that I'd seen before. I think it was black."

"Did you manage to catch a glimpse of whoever was driving?"

"Yeah. It was a woman, but I didn't get a good look at her face."

"Young or old? Blonde, brunette?" he pressed.

Dorothy shrugged. "I really couldn't tell you. You're lucky I remember the car at all."

"What made you remember it?"

"You mean besides the fact that there are only about three cars that go to the Widow Maker with any consistency?" She laughed.

He chuckled. It was one of those realities of country living that he equally hated and loved—especially when it came to his investigations. He could always go to the neighbors in a remote rural place. Someone usually saw something.

"I guess what drew my attention," Dorothy continued, "was that the woman had a pair of red Ariats in the window."

"Ariats?" he asked.

"You know," she said, motioning to her feet. "Cowboy boots. I think they were Fatbabies. I've been wanting a pair. They have a blue pair down at the ranch-supply store I think I may have to go pick up."

"Oh, they are cute," Gwen added. "They're the ones with the thick soles, right?"

"Yep. And the ones in the car window were very nice. You know, if you're into red boots." Dorothy gave a raise of the brow as she glanced over at Gwen, like the color of the boots made them obscene.

"Oh, I like red boots. Sometimes," Gwen said with a little laugh and a dismissive wave.

"Do either of you know anyone who would wear those kind of boots?"

Dorothy shrugged. "No one comes to my

mind, but then again, I don't get out of my house much. You know how it is."

Wyatt smiled. "I appreciate your help, and hey." He reached into his pocket and pulled out a business card and handed it to her. "If you think of anything else, or if you see the car again, please don't hesitate to give me a call."

She took the card and, giving it a quick glance, stuffed it into her back pocket. No doubt if Dorothy wanted to tell him something, he would probably hear it from his mother long before he would hear it from her. In fact, it was more than likely that his mother would get a call from her friend before he was even out and onto the main road.

He gave Dorothy an appreciative nod as he got into the patrol unit.

"What was going on with the whole red boots thing?" he asked, easing the car out of the driveway and toward the road that led into the small town.

"My mother used to have red boots." Gwen smiled. "And that neighbor and I… Let's just say that if she never saw my mug again she wouldn't miss it. I've had to rescue her from my screaming mother, wearing those damned red boots, more than once."

"From your mother?"

"Sometimes, on real bad nights, she forgets we've sold the place." Gwen shifted in the seat as she reached down and took out a lipstick from her purse and applied it without looking in the mirror. "Once," she said, "she thought that the woman living there was seeing my father."

"She thought your dead father was having an affair?"

She nodded. "Our neighbor really didn't appreciate getting woken up at 2:00 a.m. when my mother accused her of being a slut."

The pink color of her lipstick made her face brighten with color, and for a second he wondered if she'd put it on in an effort to look even more beautiful for him. He pushed the thought aside. She wouldn't be trying to impress him. Not after everything they'd been through. Yet as he looked at her, she smiled, and there was a new softness in her eyes.

She sighed. "I'm not sure, but I think toward the end, my father may have been going behind my mother's back. She had been drinking before he died, but it didn't take a dark turn until he was gone. And I can't take my mother's word on this kind of thing... Half of it is real and half of it... Well, it's just whatever she's imagined."

"It must be so hard," Wyatt said, reaching over to put his hand on her thigh.

She looked down at his hand, but she didn't move away. Instead she put her hand on his. She started making small circles with her fingers on the back of his hand. "Is this how you do it?"

He smiled. She was doing it right and had to have known it, but he couldn't miss this chance.

He pulled the car to the side of the road, just around a bend and out of view from the nosy neighbor. "Here, let me show you."

He unbuckled his seat belt and, leaning over, reached up and cupped her face in his hands. In a slow, meticulous move he ran his thumbs over her cheekbones, rounding the motion into a smooth, small circle. Then he let his right thumb move down lower...toward those pink lips he hoped were just for him.

She leaned into his touch and pulled the thumb into her mouth, sucking on the tip in a way that told him that she was just the kind of woman he wanted in his life.

He moaned as she nibbled on the tip of his finger, and at the sound she leaned back, releasing him from her seductive hold. His body quaked to life and he tried to ignore the lust that pulsed through his veins.

Was it possible that she wanted him as badly as he wanted her? Was it a direction he wanted to go in? She had rejected him yesterday, and everything had gone askew. If they took things down this kind of road, would it be as disastrous as they had both assumed? Or did it have a chance of not being as dead-ended as they thought?

Maybe together they could build something off the connection they had once had, and both seemed to continue to feel. They could take this in a new direction, a direction leading to something far more real and meaningful than what they'd had in high school.

But it was so risky. There were so many roadblocks. None of which was more real than the fact that if he went with this, there was more than a good chance he would get his heart broken again.

She smiled, her lip brushing against his thumb. He traced the line of her lips and dropped his hand from her face.

He wanted her. He wanted this. But now wasn't the time or the place for them to make those kinds of choices. They still had to work together, and if everything went wrong again, he didn't know if he could handle the tension that would come with their attempts at having a relationship.

Besides, he was leaving. He'd be gone for about a week. A lot could happen in that time. She could remember something about him that she hated, or she could think of a new reason not to be with him. Or maybe she wouldn't like the way he communicated when he was gone. They could make a relationship in the car work, but he wasn't sure it would have a real chance when it was tested by the outside world.

He let go of her and leaned back into his seat. She looked at him, her eyes full of a familiar heat…a heat and want that he had seen those many nights in the barn. He forced himself to look away or he knew he'd fall victim to those eyes and that face. And there would be no shielding his heart from the things that he wasn't sure he was ready to feel.

"Wyatt…" She said his name in a voice barely above a whisper, and the sound made his pulse quicken.

He cleared his throat and gripped the steering wheel. He didn't want to talk about what had just happened. He didn't hold the answers.

All he had was questions. And, maybe more than anything, he didn't want to screw this up.

She started to say something, but closed her mouth as if she had thought better of it. She wiped at the corners of her lips, fixing an invisible smear, then turned to him like she was ready to come back to reality—a reality in which their feelings for each other weren't the priority.

He didn't know what to say, so he said the first thing that came to mind that didn't involve her or them or the things he wanted to do to her. "You know what? I just had an idea. You know who drives a black Audi?"

"Who?"

The name rolled around in his mouth like a foul-tasting morsel. "Monica Poe."

"You're kidding me." The tightness in Gwen's features that had come with his changing of the subject disappeared. "Everything seems to point at her. Doesn't it?"

"And sometimes, when the signs all point in one direction, it's the answer we're looking for." There was a wiggle in his gut that told him he wasn't sure if they were on the right track, but he ignored the feeling. Even if Monica wasn't the one who had drugged

Carla and been responsible for Bianca's death, she had to have been involved.

He pulled the car back onto the road. They weren't far from the antiques shop. He glanced down at the clock. It was a little early, but it was possible Monica's shop could be open.

Even though he wasn't sure about opening his heart, he reached over and opened his hand. Gwen held back for a moment, just looking at his open palm, but she finally laced her fingers with his. It wasn't that he had wanted to reject her—far from it. Maybe she understood, or maybe she was even experiencing the same confusing rush of feelings.

This time, she didn't move her fingers in those sweet little circles he now loved so much, and he didn't either.

The closed sign was still up in the little antiques shop, but the lights were on inside as they parked out front.

"Don't say anything about our investigation or what happened to your mother. Let me see if I can feel her out a little bit first. Sound good?"

Gwen nodded but didn't say anything, and he couldn't decide if he was in trouble with her again. Thankfully, as he came around her side of the car and opened the door, she looked up at him and gave him a soft smile, making some of his fears drift away.

Maybe she did understand.

As they made their way up to the front door of the shop they each kept their distance from one other.

He tapped on the cold glass of the door, the hollow sound echoing down the empty Main Street.

At the sound, Monica poked her head out from the back room of the shop and, seeing them, waved. "I'll be right there, hold on a minute!"

The nervous tone of her voice made him wonder if she was trying to hide something. He tried to control his need to just null his way inside uninvited. Sure, some of the clues in the case pointed toward her, but there wasn't much that they could actually use to prove she was behind the murder.

After a minute, Monica came out from the back room, carrying a towel as she dried her hands. She tossed the towel over her shoulder as she gave them a stiff nod and opened the door.

"How's it going, guys? I'm surprised to see you again so soon." She looked between him and Gwen, searching their faces for clues.

Her black eye was looking a bit better. Some of the swelling had subsided and now there were places on her cheek where the bruise had started to turn a lighter shade of purple. She waved for them to come in and locked the door behind them.

The shop was full of ranching knickknacks, the kinds of things that always seemed to fill the area above his mother's kitchen cabinets— baskets and rolling pins, antique teapots and little dainty cups and saucers. In fact, he was sure his mother had a water pitcher and bowl with little blue flowers that matched the set on display in the front window.

"Is there something I can help you with?" Monica asked, making him aware he hadn't really returned her greeting.

He hadn't done it on purpose, but now she seemed almost nervous with their presence.

"Sorry, just browsing…" He motioned to the blue flowered tea set in the front window. "I think Gwen's mom has something similar to that." He looked at Gwen. "Doesn't your mom have something like that?"

Gwen frowned at him. "She has some china, but I couldn't tell you what pattern it is. I think it has some pink flowers. Maybe it's Noritake or something."

"Oh, Noritake china is very nice. I have several pieces here," Monica said, walking across to the other side of the room and picking up a white teacup with dainty white flowers and a silver trim. "This is from the Lorelei collection, one of my favorites. Just the teapot in this pattern goes for around two hundred."

He had been baiting Monica for a reaction to talking openly about Carla, but instead of growing more upset, it was almost as if the conversation about dishes brought her back into her comfort zone. And if Monica was okay with talking about Gwen's mother this soon after someone had drugged her, it was more than possible Monica didn't have anything to do with the event—or she was a dang good liar.

If she was like her husband, they could be dealing with the latter.

Monica set the teacup back on the shelf and turned back to face them. As she moved, he noticed a hint of makeup masking her black eye. Maybe it hadn't really gotten better, and she had just done her best to hide what had happened.

"How's your eye doing?" he asked.

Monica reached up. "Oh, it's fine. No big thing."

"What happened?" Gwen asked, her voice soft and full of concern.

"Oh, it was nothing, just klutzy ol' me." Monica waved them off.

He'd heard that one before. "Fall down the stairs or something?"

Her eyes widened in mock surprise. "How did you know?"

Monica was never going to tell them the truth. And she was never going to give them William as the guy who had placed the punch. She was the kind of woman who would consider it her fault if a man hit her. The thought made him hate William Poe even more.

"Where's William today?" he asked as he moved around the shop, careful never to take his eyes off her face as he searched it for tells.

She stiffened at the sound of her husband's name. "He had to head to Spokane for a few days for a conference. Why?"

"Where was he on the evening of December third?"

She looked from him to Gwen. "What does this have to do with?"

"It's nothing you have to worry about. Yet," he said. "But it would be incredibly helpful if you could give me a better idea of where you and your husband have been over the last few days," he said, his tone so sweet that he could almost taste it on his tongue.

"You weren't really talking to William about the Widow Maker's taxes, were you?" Monica said, glaring at Gwen. "Does this have something to do with your sister? About her death?"

Excitement coursed through Wyatt. They were getting somewhere.

"How do you know about Bianca's death?" Wyatt pressed.

Monica's eyes were full of anger and fear— a dangerous combination. "Everyone in the town knows about Bianca."

Did Monica fish around for information because she knew what kind of man her husband was? How much did she know about him, about what he was capable of?

"And whatever you are thinking, you can stop now," Monica continued. "William's been out of town. He was only home for a couple of hours yesterday to get some clean clothes. He'd been in Bozeman, stopped in, and left for Spokane."

"What about you? Where were you on that evening?" Wyatt asked.

"Me?" Her voice was high, so much so that it came out like a mousy squeak. "I…I was at your family's ranch."

Wyatt tried to control his excitement at her revelation. "So let me get this right... You were at the site of Bianca's murder...the night it took place?"

Things just got a whole lot more interesting.

Her gaze moved to the door, like she was thinking about running. He stepped in front of her.

"I don't know anything about your sister's murder, Gwen. I swear," she said, her voice edged on pleading.

Wyatt stared at her. "If that's right, Monica, then why do I have the feeling you're not telling us the truth?"

Chapter Thirteen

Monica was in a stage-four meltdown by the time Wyatt pulled into the parking spot in front of his mother's office at Dunrovin. She was sobbing in the back seat, the sound muted by the thick layer of Plexiglas that kept him from being hit, kicked and spit on by his normal class of back seat passengers. Though he had heard his fair share of crying—usually by men—from back there as well. Yet this time, he felt a touch of empathy.

Though Monica was his prime suspect in Bianca's murder, something about the whole thing didn't fit. Most of the time, when someone was truly guilty of a crime, they either acted completely indifferent or they started rambling—and that chatter usually led to some type of admission. But this time, he had a feeling an admission of guilt wouldn't be coming. Not from the hot mess that was currently Monica Poe.

"I swear. When I was at the ranch, I was with Christina Bell the whole time," Monica said between heaving sobs. "She and I... We were playing with Winnie. I wouldn't. I'd never. I barely even knew Bianca."

Gwen turned around in the seat to look at Monica. "What's your take on red boots?"

Monica's inhaled and wiped away a tear that had slipped down her cheek. "Red boots? What are you talking about?" Her voice was hoarse from her ugly crying.

"Do you own a pair?" Gwen asked, making Wyatt proud as she passively interrogated the woman. That was his girl.

Monica shook her head. "No, I don't wear boots."

"At all?"

"No. They hurt my feet, I have high arches." She lifted her foot for them to see her shoes. They were high heels, black with a red sole, and they looked expensive, but they definitely were about as different from a pair of cowboy boots as a person could get.

"Christian Louboutins? Wow." Gwen stared

at the shoes like they were made of gold. "I've only seen those on the internet. They're beautiful."

Monica put her foot down and sat up a bit in the plastic hard-shell seat as she regained a bit of her composure.

Gwen pointed to the back. "Those are at least a thousand dollars," she whispered.

"Thirteen hundred, but I got them on sale when I was in Vegas," Monica said, reaching for her purse and taking out a small makeup compact. She dabbed at the last bit of wetness on her face before reapplying her makeup.

Something about her sudden shift in demeanor struck Wyatt as strange, but then again, nothing about the woman or her husband was completely normal. Here she was, sitting in the back of his patrol unit, wearing a pair of shoes that cost more than his first beater pickup and reapplying her makeup like she was on a trip to the mall instead of being questioned for her involvement in a murder.

Maybe she wasn't as innocent as he had begun to think. She was just as much of an enigma as Gwen, but in an entirely different way.

He got out of the car and made his way over

to Gwen's door, then Monica's to let her out.
As Monica stepped out of the car and into the
snow, she had to carefully maneuver around
some horse droppings. He chuckled, enjoying
the juxtaposition between the high-end woman's ideals and the Montana reality.

They walked into Dunrovin's main office.
His mother wasn't there, and the phone was
ringing. Hopefully it was for reservations, and
not for someone wanting to cancel after they
heard about this week's events.

Christina came out from the back of the
office, chewing on an apple as she walked
toward the phone. She didn't notice them.
"Dunrovin Guest Ranch. This is Christina,
how may I help you?"

He stood there in the door, watching as the
dark-haired woman put something in the computer and, after a couple of minutes, hung up
the phone. Normally this kind of thing was
their receptionist's job, but Whitney was nowhere to be seen.

Christina turned around and nearly jumped
as she finally saw them standing there. "Holy
crap!" She clutched at her chest, apple still
in hand. "Where did you guys come from?"

Monica stepped between her and Wyatt.

"I need you to tell Wyatt we were together the *whole* night when Bianca was murdered."

Christina frowned at him. "Are you kidding me, Wyatt? Are you seriously coming down on my Monica?" She dumped her apple in the trash and came over and wrapped her arms around Monica, as though she were shielding her from any of his accusations.

"I'm not saying or assuming Monica had anything to do with Bianca's death," he lied. "I just need to make sure I go down the list and clear everyone who could have been involved with this."

Christina let go of Monica and motioned for her to take a seat on the other side of his mother's desk. Monica sat down, gracefully crossing her legs at the ankle.

"Monica wouldn't hurt a fly." Christina waved toward her friend like she was completely affronted by the fact that he would question her.

"What about William?" Gwen asked as she leaned against the doorjamb.

Christina passed a look to Monica that told him Christina had a clue about William's reputation.

"William wasn't here. I don't know anything about him or his dealings," Christina said, still staring at Monica. "He was out of town on the night they found Bianca's body, wasn't he?"

"Could anyone account for him at that time?" Wyatt pressed.

Monica turned to him. "Look, if you think it's him, do whatever you need to do. Track his phone… Whatever. But I'm telling you he was out of town. He wasn't behind this." Anger coursed through her voice.

"How are you so sure?" Wyatt asked.

"Because…" Some of Monica's self-assurance seemed to slip away and her shoulders and back relaxed. "Look…" She sighed. "I'm tired of playing the dance-around-it game. Let's all acknowledge the elephant in the room. I know about William and Bianca. I'm not stupid. I know he *likes* other women."

Wyatt tried to keep his jaw from falling open.

"Did he do that to your face?" Gwen asked, motioning to her eye.

"It's why he's gone. After you left the other day…I confronted him about Bianca. And about *you*."

"Me? He and I? No," Gwen scoffed.

"If you knew my husband as well as I do,

you wouldn't put it past him. No offense, but he'll screw anything that walks."

"Is he going to be coming back anytime soon?" Wyatt asked.

Monica shrugged. "I have no idea. The last time something like this happened—when I found out about one of his mistresses— he stayed on the road for a couple of weeks. But with his name and reputation somewhat tied to Bianca's murder, he may come back sooner."

At least the man was smart enough to know when his butt was on the line—and that running made him look even more suspicious.

"Why did you stay with him, Monica? If you knew what he was doing with Bianca?" Gwen asked, pity flecking her voice.

Monica sighed and rested her chin on her hand. She sat in silence for a moment as if she was trying to find exactly the right answers to such a hard question. "I knew from the day I said yes at the altar that he was the kind of man who was going to seek the company of other women."

"And you still said yes?" Gwen pushed.

Wyatt wanted to make her stop prying into the woman's private life, but in truth he was just as curious about what would possess a woman to make what must have been a terribly painful compromise.

"When I met him, I was a bit lost. I didn't know what I wanted in life. I didn't know where I wanted to go. And everyone around me was getting married. It may sound shallow, but he offered so much—thanks to his family's wealth and his job. I knew I would have a life where I would never have to worry about money, I'd never want for anything... at least not anything material. If I want to travel, I book my flight. I have my independence. And I have a man who doesn't stand in my way. Ever. He appreciates his independence—and what he can do with it."

"And you aren't jealous?" Wyatt asked.

She looked over at him, her eyes tired, and he could tell she hated that she had been forced to admit the reality of her situation to them. "I signed up for this. I don't like it. But I did this to myself. It wasn't Bianca's fault she fell for him. He can be quite charming when he wants to be."

Wyatt didn't understand it at all. To him, it seemed like an impossible lie to live. He could barely even imagine the dance they must have had to do to avoid talking about the truths of their lifestyle.

Then again, he wasn't like some men. He didn't want a million women. He didn't care about a one-night stand, or the need to have a woman validate him or fulfill his physical needs. He wanted a woman who just loved him for him. One woman...the *right* woman, and he would be endlessly satisfied.

He glanced over at Gwen.

Maybe it wasn't that he wasn't like other men. Maybe it was just that he had a taste of the woman he'd really wanted and had been waiting for her to come back to him ever since.

A thought popped into his head. "Do you think any of William's *other* women would have had a problem with Bianca?"

Monica shrugged.

"How did you know he was seeing Bianca?" Gwen asked.

Monica's gaze flickered to Christina, who was looking everywhere but at Gwen.

"Did you tell her about it, Christina?" Wyatt asked.

"I just... I put it together and—" Christina started.

Monica interrupted her. "She was just being a good friend. It's a tough spot to be in, to know someone's spouse is cheating. It's a terrible position. And I appreciate her telling me and, Gwen, I understand why you didn't—especially since it was Bianca. You were in an impossible position."

"Do you know if he was seeing anyone else?" Wyatt asked.

Monica shook her head. "I don't think so. After Christina told me about the relationship, I was tuned in to his comings and goings. To be honest, I think they were in love. Every minute he wasn't working or with me, it seemed like he was with her."

"But you're not upset? That doesn't seem right," Wyatt said, trying to make sense of it all.

"I was upset, but not with her. It wasn't Bianca's fault. Like I said, I could only be mad at myself."

He wasn't sure if she was simply more emotionally evolved than he was, or if she was just a bit dead inside because of the emotional roller coaster she had been experiencing over the years. Either way, he pitied her.

"Are you done here?" Christina asked, once again coming to bat for her friend, and it made him like her even more.

He nodded. "Sure. Thanks for taking the time out of your day to answer my questions.

Would you like us to drive you back to your place, Monica?"

Monica shook her head. "I'm not getting back in a police car if I can help it. Christina, would you mind taking me back to the shop? I need to get back to work." She stood up and, as she was about to walk out, she turned back to him. "I know my life probably doesn't make any sense to you, but I promise...I had nothing to do with Bianca's death. And, as much as I sometimes hate my husband and he hates me, he's not the kind who would do something like this. Like I said, I think he loved her. And when he's in love, he can be a magnificent man."

She and Christina walked out, not bothering to look back.

He turned to Gwen. "I need to call my team and check to see if they've found anything at your place, or if they were able to pull any fingerprints. Is there anything you need to do?"

She smiled. "I could use some food. You have a terrible habit of keeping me hungry."

He laughed. "I got some...I mean, I *have* some food back at my place," he said, nearly tripping over his words with the smooth form of a teenager.

Gwen laughed, and the sound resonated

through him. It felt good to hear that sound. "Okay. Unless it's bologna. I may not be Monica with her Louboutins," she said, motioning toward the women in the ranch truck as they pulled out of the parking area, "but I do have some standards. Conglomerated pig meat is where I draw the line."

He wasn't sure, but he could have sworn there was something more in the way she looked at him. Was it that their talk about William made her remember what kind of man Wyatt *wasn't*?

When they left the office, Alli was standing outside, holding Winnie's hand.

"Wy-ant! Where you been?" Winnie threw herself around his legs.

It made his chest tighten as he was reminded how much he loved that little girl… and how badly he wanted his own.

"Hey, Winnie-girl. How goes it, dollface?" He lifted her up and gave her a hug, then dropped her back down to her feet.

"You got candy?" Winnie asked, reaching up toward his pocket with her pudgy toddler fingers.

He reached into his pocket. When he went back to his place, he'd need a refill, but luckily he had one more piece for his best bud on the ranch. "Here you go, sweetie."

Gwen sent him a warm smile as Winnie took the piece of candy from his hand.

"Thanks you, Wy-ant!" Winnie turned to her mom and lifted the candy for her to see. "Look, Mama, he gave me this." Before her mother could take it away, Winnie unwrapped the candy, popped it in her mouth and ran toward the barn.

"No running with food in your mouth, Winnie!" Alli called after her, before turning back to them. "What were you doing in there? Why was Monica here?"

It surprised him that she would care. On the other hand, his brother's ex-wife was nothing if not nosy. No doubt, within the next few hours she would have the news that Monica had arrived at the ranch in the back of his squad car spread far and wide.

"We just had to ask everyone a few questions. No big thing. Why?" Wyatt tried to remain impassive so he could read her response.

Alli shrugged, but the motion looked forced. "Do you think Monica has something to do with Bianca's death?" She looked toward the barn. "It wouldn't surprise me if she did it. She's a vile woman. I don't know how my sister likes her. She barely speaks to me any time she comes here. It's almost like she thinks she's too good for the rest of us. But if you ask me, she stinks just as much as the rest of us."

He thought about Monica's expensive appearance. She was the kind who liked to keep up her looks. No doubt, to the dirt-covered gardener in front of him, Monica was a perfect target for Alli's hate.

He didn't understand how sweet little Winnie could have come from a woman who seemed to be solely focused on her own bitterness. At least Winnie had his family—he had no idea what he would do if she ever was forced to leave because of her disaster of a mother.

"Thanks for your opinion, Alli, but Monica has been more than helpful."

"Then she's full of crap. You shouldn't trust her farther than you can throw her." Alli looked toward the parking lot.

He'd had enough. Whatever her opinions, his dislike for her erased any objectivity he should have had in listening to her. Without bothering to say goodbye, he took Gwen's hand and led her back to his patrol unit. Sometimes it was just easier to walk away from a fight in which idiocy and close-mindedness were the only things really up for debate.

Chapter Fourteen

It was a short drive to Wyatt's place, and Gwen was glad. Her stomach grumbled with hunger as she walked to Wyatt's refrigerator and opened the door. Stale air poured out at her, making her wonder exactly how much he ate at home. She smiled as she looked in at the fridge's contents. He had an old loaf of bread, a wrinkled tomato and a block of cheese sitting on the shelf. Tucked into the far corner was a stick of salami and a pint-size jar of mayonnaise.

It wasn't pretty, but she could do something with the man-ish contents of his fridge.

Wyatt walked out of the bedroom. He was still on the phone with what she assumed was the crime lab. "We could really use a rush on those fingerprints. We have a lead on a couple of suspects, but I can't make any arrests until we have conclusive results. I'd love to have everything in order before I leave." He paused. "Yep, Alaska." Another pause. "You know it. I am one lucky son of a gun. Gonna take the fishing pole! Maybe I'll bring you back some fish since we both know you can't catch any on your own." He laughed and the sound was warm and full of life.

Normally that sound would have made her body tingle, but all she could think about was Alaska. Two more days and he would be leaving for a week.

Standing there in his kitchen, she wondered what it would have been like if they hadn't ended things when they were younger. To have let things between them naturally progress instead of her cutting them down? Sure, there was no going back and changing what had already happened, but there was no harm in dreaming.

Or was it *hoping*?

She laughed, brushing back a hair from her forehead, taking out the contents of the fridge and setting about making them sandwiches.

Maybe if she ignored reality, she could pretend this is what life would have been like if they had gotten married—her puttering around their place, him working and making plans while she was taking care of them. Or if they had stayed together, maybe she could have dreamed of something bigger than being a domestic goddess.

She'd been thrust into the role of caregiver for her mother, and now that Bianca was gone, everything about the ranch would also fall into her lap. They had put the bulls out to pasture with the cows, so in the spring she would at least have a hundred new calves— and then hopefully they could sell them for enough to keep the ranch going for another year. But without Bianca here, Gwen would have to take on extra hands.

She sighed as she glanced over at Wyatt, who stood by the window looking out at his family's spread.

In all truth, she hated ranching. Most thought of it as this romantic thing, early mornings spent around a campfire drinking coffee and nights in the arms of a cowboy, but her reality was nothing like that. Her mornings were usually taken up with feedings and moving animals, her afternoons were spent cleaning and then, when an animal was sick, Bianca had stepped in. The ranch had captured her sister just as much as it had trapped her, and now that Bianca was gone, it would be so much harder.

There was no way she could do it all by herself.

Wyatt hung up the phone and walked over to the counter to stand beside her. When he didn't wrap her in his arms she was surprised by the faint wave of disappointment that filled her.

Her daydream was definitely not the same as her reality. Then again, when had her dreams ever come true?

"Would you ever want to go back into ranching?" she asked, in hope that somehow their stars would align.

"I don't mind ranching. But I like what I do. Why?" He pulled open a drawer and, taking out a knife, set to spreading mayonnaise on the bread.

She could hardly tell him that she was feeling him out, or that she was praying he would help her make sense of her life and what she hoped was their future.

"That's great that you like your job," she said, in an attempt to maneuver around her fears.

"Do you like ranching?" he asked with a quirk of his brow.

She took a long breath as she sliced the salami and set it on the bread he'd prepared. "It's a lot. There's so much I should be doing right now, especially now that it's winter. We're close, but I want to get one more pass on the fences before more snow falls."

"If you need help now that, you know, everything's changed." He was careful about not saying what they were both thinking—that she was lost without Bianca.

She chewed on the inside of her cheek as she stared at the counter. "I might need to bring on another hand. We'll have to see. Right now, with just me, it's tough and it's only going to get harder. Then again, we can't really afford anything. Things are tight."

As soon as she admitted the truth, she wished she could take it back. He wasn't anything more than a friend. He didn't need to add her struggles to his plate. He needed to stay at surface level when it came to the real things going on in her life.

"Why are you keeping the ranch?" He reached over and took a piece of the meat and popped it into his mouth.

She had given thought to that question a thousand times, each time she and Bianca had been forced to sell bits of their ranch in an effort to keep everything afloat. Each time, she'd come back to the same conclusion— she didn't want to be the generation that let it crumble. The Widow Maker had been in her family for four generations. Each generation had their own obstacles—both financial and personal—that had made it nearly impossible to keep the ranch, but no matter how bad things got, they had always managed to make it work.

She couldn't be the one to fail.

"There's no shame in selling it," Wyatt continued, thankfully not waiting for her to answer.

He didn't know how weak she felt, or how out of control. And how, if she put her thoughts of possibly failing out into the world, she feared they would be what came to be.

"There is shame in it, Wyatt." She handed him his sandwich and took a bite of her own.

He watched her as she took another bite. "How are you going to run that place on your own? I mean, it's a huge job. You never even really seemed to like this kind of life. Isn't there something you'd rather be doing? Something that you *really* want?"

She set the sandwich down. The one thing she *really* wanted was him. She wanted to be his everything. She wanted for them to get married. To travel around the world and be as free as the wind. Then, when they were ready, she would love to have kids—to see him light up like he did whenever he saw Winnie. She would love to be wholly consumed by their reality.

Maybe what she wanted most was to be truly, completely happy. No matter what job she did or where life placed her, she didn't care. She could be satisfied. But she had a sinking feeling that the only way to have true happiness was to find it with the man standing beside her.

"You know what I really want?" Her voice was soft and sultry and she moved toward him. "I want you..." She reached up and ran her fingers through his hair.

The sandwich in his hand came to full a stop at his lips. He smiled and swallowed the bite in his mouth. He stared at her like he was trying to figure her out, but there was really no need. She had said what she had meant.

She took the sandwich from him and sat it on the counter beside hers. Wiping the crumbs from the corners of his lips, he turned toward her and pulled her into his arms. His kiss was hard, and she grabbed his hair with both of her hands, pressing him against her lips even harder, until all they had was each other, their breaths on each other's skin and the taste of salt on their tongues.

He growled as his hands slipped down and he cupped her ass. He squeezed, and she pulled back as she giggled. His brown eyes were full of heady lust.

Maybe he wasn't as unsure about this as he had seemed before. He probably was still at the "it would be great, but" stage, yet right now she didn't care. Not when she could have him like she had wanted to for so long.

He reached down and lifted her up, wrapping her legs around him. She kissed his neck, taking in the flavor of his skin and the aroma of fresh air he always seemed to exude.

"Where are you taking me?" She hugged his neck.

"Where would you like to go, my lady?" he said with a sexy half smirk.

"Hey now, who said I was a lady?" She gave him a sexy quirk of the brow.

"You are one, but for the sake of argument, if you're not a lady…" He sat her down on the counter and pushed all the sandwich-making supplies to the floor with a one-armed swipe.

"Someone is going to have to clean that up," she said with a laugh.

"Don't worry about it. I've been on my own for a long time. I'm more than capable of cleaning up," he said, pulling her close so that she could feel his body's response against her.

His heat mixed with hers, making the desire she had been feeling seem that much more raw and urgent. She reached down. At least this time he wasn't wearing his utility belt like he had before the shower—it would be a little less work to get what she wanted, and it would give them each less time to think of the hundred reasons they shouldn't be doing what they were.

He took hold of her hand and she stopped moving. "Are you sure?" he asked, leaning in so his hot breath caressed her earlobe.

She looked up at him and their eyes met. "We should have done this a long time ago. I can't believe all the time we wasted." She took his lips, kissing him as her fingers went back to work opening his fly.

He was rock hard in her hand, and for a moment she considered just playing with him and stroking him until he couldn't stand it any longer. She moved her hand over him. He felt so good that she could only imagine how he would feel in other, more forbidden places.

She couldn't stand the thought of waiting a minute longer.

He pulled back slightly, almost as if they were of one mind. He reached down, unbuttoned her pants and, in one smooth motion, pulled them from her and let them fall to the floor. He ran his fingers up her thighs, making her moan as his fingers trailed over the outside of her panties.

He moved to her hip and, taking the panties, he ripped them. "I hope you weren't fond of this pair."

She shook her head. All that she could think about was the way he moved the fabric against her, making her think of all the things she wanted him to do and all the places she wanted him to explore.

There was the crinkle of a wrapper as he pulled a condom from his pants pocket and ripped it open, and then slipped it on.

She didn't let him take the time to pull off her shirt; instead, reaching down, she pulled him to her. Some things just couldn't wait. Her body was one of them.

As he moved into her, he groaned, making the feeling all that much more pleasurable. There had never been a sweeter sound. He moved slowly, letting her body grow accustomed to the full feeling of him inside her. She wasn't one who was fast to completion... usually. Yet, he felt so good—far better than she had ever imagined.

There were so many times when their communication had failed, but apparently their bodies didn't have the same problem. It was as if, before he even moved, she knew what he was going to do, and she moved her body in a way that drove him deeper, harder and into places that promised a quick end.

She ran her fingers through his hair, pulling his short locks. He moaned as he grew impossibly harder inside her. He kissed her neck. His hot breath came in the same cadence as the movement of his body.

It was all too much.

This reality was much better than any daydream.

HE COULDN'T BELIEVE it had happened. Twice.

He'd spent so many nights thinking about what it would feel like to have her wrap her body around him, to feel her warm, naked skin on his. Every imagining he'd ever had paled in comparison to the real thing. She had been perfect. Everything about her, even when he'd lifted her from the counter to find a piece of bread stuck to her back.

They'd both laughed as he pulled it off and threw it into the sink before carrying her to the bedroom.

They had been at it for so long that somewhere along the way it had turned to night and the cool air caught his cheap curtains and made them flutter in the breeze. He traced his fingers down her arm; her skin was cold under his touch, so he pulled his quilt over her. There was no way he would disturb her slumber just to get up and close the window. Not in a moment as perfect as this.

He played with the ends of her hair, lifting the strands and twisting them between his fingers, then letting them fall softly back down to her skin. She had always had the same hairstyle, the same long and flowing locks pulled half up and out of her face. Only the color had changed, growing darker over the years from a nearly white-blond to the honey color it was now. As he rolled another strand around his finger, he thought about all the other things that had changed about her as well, and what would change now that their relationship had grown.

Hopefully when she woke up and thought about what they had done, she wouldn't regret it.

He thought back to when he'd been a kid. Now he understood that his mother's addiction and the problems she had faced weren't his fault. Yet as a child, he'd always tried to be perfect, to protect the people who needed it and to make himself worthy of their love. Most of the time, he had fallen short—and with his mother, it had ended with her losing him. She had never come to look for him, and he'd never felt really worthy of being loved. Not when there were so many things that were broken within him—and not when he'd always continue to make mistakes.

Hopefully over time Gwen could just learn to love his imperfections instead of hating him for them. Maybe someday he could show her how worthy he was of her love. There would always be mistakes, but if they were supposed to be with each other they would make it work.

His mind went to their investigation and the list of mistakes he could be making there, and the things he feared he had missed.

He couldn't get the thoughts of Monica and her possible role in his investigation out of his mind. She was guilty of something—well, something more than just putting up with a less-than-ideal spouse. She was hiding something. Just because she didn't own red boots, that didn't mean she was innocent. Maybe she had them in the window of her car for someone else. Or who knew, maybe the neighbor had been wrong and there weren't even boots in the window. Witnesses had been wrong before.

Monica had sworn her innocence and given a testimony about not having feelings of ill will toward Bianca...but she had been at the right place at the right time and she had the right motive. All she had to do was tell Christina she was going to the restroom or something, then slip out and jab the needle in Bianca's neck. It wouldn't have been hard. Hell, she could have done it on a whim, just as he had assumed.

He thought of Carla. Who knew why Monica would have gone after the woman. Maybe she simply hated her. Or maybe Carla had found out about Bianca and William and had threatened to blackmail the Poes. There were a thousand possible reasons that Monica could have for wanting Carla dead.

Just because she had paid him a little bit

of lip service didn't mean she was actually innocent. He needed the results from those damned forensics idiots. Or he was going to have to find something else to definitively pin the crime to her.

Gwen sighed in her sleep.

If anything, she was proof there were angels out there. She fought and tried so hard. Maybe things could start going her way.

He closed his eyes, willing himself to go to sleep. He would need all his faculties tomorrow if he was going to get this all figured out. Time was ticking away.

He lay there in the dark, listening to the sound of her breath and feeling her heartbeat against his side as she lay curled up beside him. He basked in the feeling of her against him as he slipped in and out of sleep.

Just outside the open window, there was the crunch of snow and the sound of footsteps. They stopped suddenly.

Wyatt stiffened as he listened for the sound again. There were only the comforting sounds of Gwen and the echo of his heartbeat in his ears.

There was something, or *someone*, outside. He would swear on it.

He tried to control his breathing. In and out. Slow.

Then, in the window, profiled by the moon, was a person. As Wyatt jumped to his feet and ran toward the window, the petite shadow disappeared.

Chapter Fifteen

Who would have been spying on them, and why?

Gwen stared out at the spot where Wyatt had said the person had escaped into the shadows. He'd sworn the person had only looked in at them for a moment, but who knew how long they had been watching or what they had seen. The thought made her skin crawl.

Wyatt walked into the bedroom. He was already dressed in his full uniform, belt and all, and he carried two cups of coffee. He handed her one. The cream swirled in the mug, and for a second she wondered where it could have possibly come from as she recalled the woefully lacking contents of his fridge.

"Why didn't you wake me up?" she asked, motioning toward the window. "We could have gone after them."

"Whoever it was, they were quick. And who knows, maybe I was just seeing things. Maybe I was just tired."

She could hear the lie in his voice.

Taking a sip of the hot coffee, she let the lie disappear into the waves of silence between them. The coffee was sweet, with a touch of almond, and she loved the fact that she had found a man who knew his way around a coffeepot. There was a lot to be said for a guy who could make a decent cup of joe.

"Who do you think it could have been?" she asked, moving around his attempt to protect her once again. "Do you think it was the murderer? Or do you think it was just someone from the ranch being nosy?"

He snorted. "I thought of that. If anyone saw you come home with me last night, they might have wanted to know where things had ended up. But I don't think there's anyone here crazy or desperate enough to stand outside my window to find out."

She realized exactly how much of what had happened seemed to be tied to Dunrovin. Even the drugging of her mother had been after Mrs. Fitz's appearance at their house.

Then again, it was all circumstantial. Plenty of other things had happened: Bianca's hate mail from the library, her cabin and clinic being turned over and the picture being stolen… Maybe Gwen was just tuned in to the ranch right now, and the connection meant nothing.

She didn't understand how Wyatt could want to do a job that required thoughts like this all day, every day. It felt as though she was going through a special kind of emotional and mental torture. Everyone was a possible suspect, and everywhere she turned, she feared what she would find. This was his reality.

"For all I know, it was just a deer. I don't think it's anything you should worry about," he said.

"Huh. Okay," she said, setting down the mug on his dresser before grabbing her pants, which he had neatly folded over the chair in the corner. She slipped them on. They felt strange against her nakedness, but she liked the way it reminded her of what they had done.

Wyatt watched as she slipped on her clothes, but said nothing, only amplifying the awkwardness she felt.

"You know…" she started, then paused. "You don't have to protect me all the time.

You don't have to keep the truth from me. I'm a tough girl."

She glanced over at him, there was a slight look of shock and hurt on his face.

"I'm…I know you're strong," he stammered. "But here's the thing," he tried again with a sigh. "You are one of the strongest women I know. But with everything going on, I'm not going to let anything happen to you. For all we know, the person who came here last night came with the intention to hurt you."

"So you *admit* there was someone outside the window?" She motioned to the glass. "What did you find?"

He gave a resigned sigh. He reached down and pulled his phone from his utility belt. He clicked a few times and then lifted the screen so she could see it.

There, in the photo, was a set of footprints in the thin layer of snow. He enlarged the photo so she could see it more clearly.

"That," he said, "is a set of boot prints. If you look right here at the center of the boot—" he pointed to the spot "—that is the symbol for the Ariat brand."

The killer *had* been outside the window. The realization hit her like a fist to the gut. Wyatt was right. Whoever had come after her mother and killed her sister had come for her too.

What had she ever done to deserve being hunted down like an animal?

"Do you…do you really think they were here to hurt me?"

Wyatt stuffed the phone back on his belt. "I don't know. And we can't know for sure, Gwen, but what I do know is that I'm not going to leave you alone. Not until this bastard is behind bars."

She didn't want to ask him about Alaska. What would happen when he went north? What if they didn't get whoever was behind this? Would she be killed next?

He took a long drink of his coffee. "I was hoping we could look into Monica a little more today and see if we can get any further with our investigation. Her shop should be open. If we get over there, maybe we can talk to her before customers start showing up."

"But I thought you had already cleared her? She had an alibi."

"She did, but she and Christina were two of only a few who might have known you were at my place last night." Wyatt walked out of the bedroom toward the kitchen.

"That doesn't mean it was her at the window." Gwen grabbed her coffee and followed him, guzzling down the rest of the creamy goodness. She would need as much coffee as she could get to handle the rest of the day.

"No, but maybe she called someone...or maybe she hired someone to take you all down." He set his coffee cup in the kitchen sink and turned back to her. "She knows something more than she is telling us. And I intend to figure out what she's holding back, and why."

Gwen wasn't sure why he was so adamant. When they'd seen Monica, it had gone better than she had expected—though she was still surprised by Monica's admission about her knowledge of William's affairs.

She could never live a life where she would compromise her principles like that just to keep her social life in working order. Nothing was more important than being happy—no amount of money, number of friends or material goods could make up for the constant pain that came with a broken heart.

Gwen set her cup in the sink beside his and took one last look around his place before she followed him outside. It was a terrible thought, but as she closed the door, she couldn't help but wonder if this would be the last time she would be in Wyatt's house…if she had just reached the pinnacle of her life and everything now was going downhill.

HE HAD TO get to the bottom of this murder, and fast. He had called his sergeant, but things hadn't gone as he'd hoped. Wyatt had tried to convince him to send another officer to handle the prisoner transfer in Alaska, but his sergeant was having none of it. In fact, he'd made it more than clear that not following his orders would only end with Wyatt getting kicked off the force. Would it be worth it? Losing everything to protect the woman he had always loved?

He had twenty-four hours to find the person they were looking for.

He pulled into a parking spot down the street from the door of the antiques shop. Gwen's face was tight, but her fingers were loose in his hand. What he would give to go back to last night when everything in life had been forgotten and they had just lived in the bliss of one another's bodies.

He walked to her side of the car and stood there for a moment, looking in at her and at the soft, full contours of her lips. He had kissed that spot last night, and he wished he could kiss that spot again. But in the middle of the morning traffic moving down Main Street and people rushing toward their jobs, it just didn't seem like a good time to start kissing the woman in the front seat of his patrol unit.

He opened her door. "You look beautiful," he said in an attempt to make the tautness around her lips disappear.

She smiled and it made some of the aching in his chest fade.

Even if he didn't have a clue what his next move should be, at least the rest of his steps today would be made with her at his side. If only the same could be said for the rest of his life. He loved his job, but if he could just have her, nothing else really mattered.

Yet he was sure if he told her about the decision he was poised to make about his job, she'd never let him give up what he had worked so hard to achieve. No matter how forlorn she seemed any time they'd spoken about his going to Alaska, he was certain she'd never want him to do anything to put his career in jeopardy. On the other hand, he wasn't prepared to put her life in jeopardy by leaving either.

He helped her out of the car and watched her walk in front of him to the antiques shop.

He should have been thinking about the questions he needed to ask Monica, but all he could concentrate on was the way Gwen looked in her jeans. She no longer had the high and tight behind that she'd had at sixteen, but she had become perfect in her soft curves. Curves he had loved running his hands over when she was on top of him. He stopped moving and just stood there, staring as she walked ahead with a quiet grace of a woman confident with her body. As she shifted her hips, he wondered if she was doing it on purpose just in case he was watching.

He smiled and looked up just as she stopped to wait for him.

"What are you doing?" she asked with a coy smile.

She *had* played it up for him.

"Nothing," he said with a quirk of his brow. "I was just taking a sec to enjoy the view. Feel free to keep walking."

She giggled as she sauntered back to him and took him by the hand. He looked around. A few of the older women were looking over at him, and he wondered how long it would take for word to spread that he and Gwen were officially an item. He smiled and gave the woman closest to them a quick, acknowledging wave. The woman nodded but quickly turned away.

He didn't care if the world knew. He'd waited so long for this, so long to be with the one woman who had filled his thoughts during the day and his dreams in the night. ¬

Gwen stroked his fingers and gave them a quick kiss as they turned toward the store. As her lips left his fingers, he finally looked up. The lights of the store were off, and even though Secret Secondhand should have been open, the closed sign was still flipped in the window of the front door.

Wyatt glanced down at his watch. It was nearly 10:00 a.m. Monica wasn't the kind to be late. Ever. She was entirely too perfect to be an hour late opening the store.

Something was wrong.

He stepped up and pressed his face against the cold glass of the front door, shielding the morning sun from his eyes. The store was a mess. The glass teapot, the one he had noticed the day before, was on the floor, shattered into pieces. Beside it was a bloody handprint. Next to the counter was a large pool of blood.

It felt like the world was collapsing around him. He glanced back at Gwen. She didn't need to see this, but he couldn't keep her from the truth…or what they might find if they went into the shop. He needed to get in, clear the building and get help if there was someone hurt inside. And yet, he had promised himself he wouldn't let her be alone again.

"Gwen…" he said, turning around to face her.

"What's wrong?" she asked. All the playfulness she had been exuding disappeared.

"I need to go in there. Something's happened."

"To Monica?"

He shrugged. "I can't be sure until I look."

"What do you want me to do?"

He could make her wait in the car, but just because she was in his car didn't mean she'd be entirely safe. Whoever was gunning for her had to be someone they both knew, someone close to them, and it was likely someone who could lure her out.

He couldn't risk it.

Though he had a feeling that it was unlikely they had arrived in time to help whomever the blood belonged to, he notified dispatch and requested that they send an ambulance.

He twisted the shop's doorknob, but it was locked.

"Follow me," he said, taking Gwen by the

hand and leading her around to the back of the building.

Her hand was sweaty in his, but he couldn't tell if it was her sweat or his. Normally he would have been fine in this situation, he would have easily gone into work mode, but he couldn't let his emotions go. Not when he was holding the hand of the person he cared about most in this world. If something happened to her, he would never forgive himself.

The back door was wide-open. The alley behind the store was empty except for a large blue Dumpster and an orange tabby cat that quickly scurried out of sight. The alley muffled the sounds from the street and the muted effect made chills run down his spine.

"No matter what happens, you need to stay back. Got it?" He couldn't help the darkness that flecked his tone.

He squeezed her fingers and then let her go. Drawing his gun, he made his way up the steps. He charged the door, stopping with his gun drawn as he flagged the room. The back of the shop was empty except for shelf after shelf of dust-covered knickknacks. He looked back at Gwen and waved for her to follow him.

Her eyes were wide with fear as she stared

at him, but he couldn't let her fear get to him any more than it already had. He had to keep them safe and he had to do it by being prepared and taking the lead.

"Lake County sheriff's deputy! Come out with your hands up!" he ordered.

They were met with a sickening silence.

"Monica Poe, are you in here?" he called again.

There was no answer.

The hair rose on the back of his neck.

He silently prayed that his intuition was wrong and that Monica was okay.

He lowered his Glock as he moved forward and toward the main area of the store.

Next to the doorway was a smashed clock in the shape of a black-and-white cat. The jovial cat's face looked up at him, and right between the eyes was a droplet of blood.

There was another spatter of blood as he stepped inside the room. A cabinet full of glass ornaments had been pushed over and he stepped around it, the glass crunching under his shoes.

There was a smear of blood on the floor, where it looked as though someone had crawled toward the front desk.

"Wait here," he said, motioning for Gwen to

stop and stay out of the crime scene as much as possible.

He moved toward the front desk. A pair of feet with black high heels poked out from behind it. The shoes had red bottoms. Christian Louboutins.

"Monica?" he asked, but he knew it was too late.

She wouldn't respond to her name.

She wouldn't answer to anything ever again.

He stepped around the desk. Her hair was wrapped around her face, almost obscuring her open, sightless eyes. Blood pooled around her. So much blood.

Her neck had been cut so deep that he could see the white viscera of her severed windpipe. Whoever had wielded the weapon had been vicious. It was the kind of savage attack that came from a place of deep-seated hate.

He'd seen death at least a hundred times, but this was the first time he'd ever been forced to turn away.

Out of the corner of his eye, he spotted a print. One solitary boot print, each groove and line perfectly preserved and captured, thanks to Monica's blood.

Chapter Sixteen

There was a crowd of people outside the store and everyone was trying to get to Gwen to ask her their questions. Wyatt was standing next to a reporter who was holding up a microphone so close to his face that Wyatt had to remind himself to breathe.

He hated this part of his job, when he had to play to the media. They wanted to know every detail, and in cases like this, details were in high demand and short supply.

It wasn't every day something like this happened in Mystery.

He really felt worse for Gwen. She wasn't used to this kind of thing, and as the reporters descended on her, she looked like a shivering puppy. He tried to get closer to her, but the reporter stepped between them and raised the microphone higher.

"Deputy Fitzgerald, it has come to our attention that you are the lead investigator on the Bianca Johansen murder case. Do you believe your involvement is a conflict of interest since the murder happened on your family's ranch?"

It was low, but as Wyatt ignored the annoying reporter and moved past him, he did his best to step on the toe of the man's well-polished leather loafers.

Who did he think he was? He didn't tell the reporter how to do his job. What gave the reporter the gumption to come at him like he had no business taking this case?

"Out of the way," Wyatt said, elbowing the man as he grabbed Gwen by the hand and led her out of the crowd.

Another officer pushed the reporter back as the guy tried to move after them and cast another net of questions. "Everyone back!" the officer ordered. "This is an active crime scene! We would appreciate your keeping your distance until we have finished our investigation. At that time you are welcome to reach out to our public information officer and they will provide an official statement. Until then, go on about your day!"

A few of the people turned away, but they didn't move off the sidewalk.

Wyatt was filled with disgust. Normally he didn't mind living in a small town, where everything was fair game for the rumor mill, but right now he just wished the crowd would leave him alone.

An officer walked toward them as he finally helped Gwen out of the melee. "Fitz, I think you may want to step inside," the officer said, motioning toward the shop. "We found something."

Gwen glanced at him with a look begging him not to leave her.

"Gwen's coming with us," he said to the officer. He turned toward her. "You don't have to stay out here with the vultures."

She relaxed. He was glad he could be there for her, that she needed him…and truth be told, he liked it.

The officer led them up the steps, through the creaking door and into the front area of the store, carefully avoiding the body that was now being photographed and documented. He was glad Gwen didn't have to look at her friend's body. She hadn't taken it well, and he didn't want to put her back in that kind of position again.

He turned to her. "Do you want to wait here?"

She stared over in the direction of the front desk, where Monica's body lay just out of view. She didn't say anything, but gave him a slow, stiff nod.

"We haven't called Monica's husband yet," the other officer said, walking with him toward the desk. "I know that you're acquainted with the family..."

They were trying to pass the buck. Not that he could blame them. He glanced back over at Gwen. She had her arms pulled tight around her body. The memory of her lying on the floor, crying after he had told her of Bianca's death, came to mind. William Poe wasn't Gwen, but Wyatt had had more than his fair share of notifying the next of kin for a while.

Besides, he cringed at the thought of what William would say when he found out about his wife. Though, would it come as a surprise? It was possible that William had a hand in this.

"I'll get someone to take care of it," Wyatt said. "Now, what did you guys find?"

The officer walked over to him. Lyle was standing beside the cash register, his round belly pressing against his shirt and pulling the buttons open. He hitched up his pants, giving a break to his struggling suspenders. "How's it going, man?"

"It's going. Heard you found something?" Wyatt couldn't help the little bit of surprise that filled his tone.

Lyle raised a brow, like he'd heard the unintentional jab as well.

Wyatt started to open his mouth to apologize, but Lyle turned around before he had the chance to speak.

"By the way, I'm real sorry about missing the syringe…but you know what they say about a needle in a haystack," Lyle said with a laugh. "And we did manage to pull some fingerprints from that vet bag, but they ain't comin' up in the database. We'll keep tryin', though. However, look what I just found…" Lyle lifted the cash register. Underneath was a white envelope. He pulled it out and handed it over to Wyatt. "There's some interesting stuff in there. In fact, I'd like to think it might just break your case wide-open."

He wasn't sure he believed the guy.

Wyatt flipped open the envelope and a series of pictures slid out. On the top was a photo of Bianca. She was standing in her cabin, wearing only a black lace teddy. Wyatt instinctively looked away. It felt so wrong seeing her like that, in a private moment meant only for the person she was with. Without looking too closely, he flipped to the next picture. It was of a brunette woman, her head down in William Poe's lap and her face completely out of view. Even from behind, he could tell by the hair color it wasn't Bianca. Picture after picture was William Poe with a different woman.

"What do you think? Gonna help your case?" Lyle asked.

Wyatt looked up from the pictures. "Why would Monica have these?"

Lyle shrugged. "If I had to guess I'd say she's been keeping an eye on her husband's bedroom activities. From the pics it looks like there's been plenty of 'em." The man chuckled.

He wasn't wrong about that. Wyatt wasn't even a third of the way through the pictures. There had to be at least forty of them. His thoughts went back to what Monica had told him about William's relationship with Bianca—and how William had slowed down when it came to dating other women. Seeing these, it was no wonder she knew exactly what had been going on as far as his affairs.

He flipped to the next picture. There,

standing in front of William, bent over, was a woman in red boots. Red. Ariat. Boots. The woman's face was down, but she was small. Just like the person he'd seen in his window.

He tried to see anything that would give away the woman's identity, but there was nothing beside the boots and her naked body for reference. There were no visible tattoos, no birthmarks or piercings. He lifted the photo for Lyle to see. "You know who this woman may be?"

Lyle shook his head. "No, but William had good taste." He chuckled, but Wyatt didn't think there was anything funny about the picture, or the woman in it.

The woman in the photo had to be the killer.

He flipped to the next picture.

She was there again. This time she was standing in the middle of a hotel room wearing nothing but those damned red boots. She was smiling, almost as if she knew there was someone right outside the window taking the picture.

It was the smile of someone who knew they were guilty—and didn't care.

It was the smile of Alli Fitzgerald.

Chapter Seventeen

The parking lot at Dunrovin was full of guests' cars. They ranged from old beat-up trucks like hers to high-end sports cars. As they got out of Wyatt's squad car, for the first time since she'd been working with him, he didn't come around to open her door. He was a man on a mission.

How could they not have seen Alli was behind this? It all made sense. She had been at the ranch. It would have been all too easy for her to get the drop on Bianca. Bianca would have trusted her. She probably wouldn't have thought anything of the woman coming into the barn. If anything, maybe Bianca had thought she had come to help.

Deep, burning hate filled Gwen. Bianca hadn't done anything to Alli, and yet Alli had come after her. All because of a man and what

Gwen had to assume was jealousy. Alli must have wanted him all to herself.

A lump grew in Gwen's throat as she tried to keep her anger and tears in check.

Her sister had fallen in love with the wrong man, but who hadn't made a mistake when it came to love? Love wasn't an emotion that made sense. It wasn't something that could be controlled or put in a vacuum.

She glanced over at Wyatt as he strode through the parking lot, and she rushed to keep up.

Once someone had told her that there was no such thing as a selfless act. She couldn't disagree more. Being in love was the most selfless act anyone could ever undertake. Just like with Bianca. She had given up who she was and what she believed in in order to be with a man. In the end, that love, that need to be with the person her heart yearned for, had cost her everything—even her life.

Winnie ran out of the barn toward them. "Wy-ant!" she called, waving wildly.

Wyatt rushed over to the little girl and pulled her into his arms, the action so protective that it made Gwen wonder if he feared for the girl's safety. Alli wouldn't do anything to put her daughter at harm. Then again, she already had—she had murdered. Twice. And she'd tried to kill Gwen's mother.

Gwen stopped and just stared as Winnie hugged Wyatt's neck. The girl reached into his shirt pocket without asking and pulled out her beloved banana taffy.

Why *had* Alli tried to kill Gwen's mother? There was no way William Poe would go after her. She wasn't his type. The attack couldn't have been motivated by jealousy. So why?

It didn't make sense.

"Where's your mama, Ms. Winnie?" Wyatt asked.

"Which one?" Winnie asked, ripping open the candy's wrapper and popping the little morsel into her mouth.

"Huh?" Wyatt asked, walking with her in his arms toward the main office. "What do you mean by 'which one,' sweetheart?"

"Mama say she not my mommy no more. Mommy gone. Christina's mommy now." Winnie was surprisingly nonchalant about her mother's sudden disappearance.

When Gwen had been a young child, if her mother would have disappeared, she would have been distraught. Then again, those had been the days when her mother was sober and almost normal. And maybe Winnie's age, added to the fact that she had no concept of time, was the reason she didn't understand the ramifications. Maybe to her, as young as she was, she thought of her mother's disappearance as if it was nothing more than her mother going to the grocery store.

Gwen was going to be without a sister forever, but she wasn't the only one who had lost someone.

"Have you seen your grandmother?" Wyatt asked, bouncing Winnie gently in his arms.

Winnie shrugged, sucking the stickiness off her fingers.

What Gwen would give to go back to those days, when life was easy, things were simpler and she had spent her days ranking which candy was best. Even with everything going on, the thought made her smile. She loved Winnie. She couldn't understand how her mother would just leave her behind.

Maybe it was just another example of love—maybe Alli knew her life was a mess and giving her daughter to her sister was the one selfless thing she could do to make things right for the girl.

The lights in the office were off, so they made their way to the main house. The wooden steps that led to the front door creaked as they walked up—the sound was disquieting and it made the hair stand to attention on Gwen's arms.

Before they could even get to the door, Mrs. Fitzgerald opened it. "We heard about Monica. Are you guys okay?"

Gwen nodded as Wyatt stepped inside with Winnie. He set the girl down. "Stay close. Okay, sweetheart?"

Winnie nodded, but she turned toward the kitchen before the words were even completely out of his mouth.

"There are homemade cinnamon rolls on the stove. Your auntie is in there and can help you," Eloise called after the girl.

"So, what did you hear?" he asked, turning to his mother.

"About Monica? Just that she was found dead in her store. Why? What happened?"

"Have you seen Alli?"

Eloise shook her head. "Why?"

"Do you know what kind of car she drives?" Wyatt asked, motioning toward the parking lot.

"She just bought a new little black Genesis, why?"

Wyatt's face fell. "Son of a… When did she buy it?"

"I don't know. She and I aren't that close. Maybe a week or two ago?"

Gwen turned to him. "Can we put out a BOLO on her?"

Wyatt nodded. "We can try, but I have a feeling that with all the roads around here..." He looked down at his watch. "If she's smart, she's already in Canada by now."

Wyatt's phone rang. His face tightened as he looked at it. It was his sergeant.

"Sir?" he answered.

Even from where she stood, she could hear the husky voice of Wyatt's superior. "Did you find the woman yet?"

Wyatt rubbed his hand over his face. "Not yet. She and her car are missing. I need to put out a BOLO on a new black Hyundai Genesis. Temporary tags."

"I'll handle it," the sergeant said. "But are you sure she is the one behind this? What exactly do you have that ties her to the case?"

Gwen's stomach sank. She didn't know much about police procedures. Everything pointed to Alli—even the woman's sketchy behavior made her seem guilty—but the only real evidence they had was a pair of red boots and a few compromising pictures.

"We're pretty sure it's her. She was in the

pictures. There were boot prints outside my window. It had to be her. She had the motivation and the opportunity to have been behind all these deaths."

"But you don't have a witness. The DA is going to have a field day when they run us through the ringer on this one—even if we do find Alli. And if we don't..."

A witness. They needed a witness.

Gwen gasped, the sound so sharp that Wyatt stared at her.

"What about my mother?"

"What about her?"

"What if she saw something? What if that's the reason Alli came after her?"

Wyatt gave her a sexy half grin and lifted the phone higher on his ear. "You send the guys after Alli."

CARLA WAS SITTING up in her bed, pale and sweaty, jittery from the effects of detox and coming down off the ample supply of drugs that had been filtered through her system over the last few days.

"How are you feeling?" Gwen asked, walking into the hospital room with Wyatt at her side.

They stopped beside her mother's bed, and

Wyatt shifted his weight from one foot to the other, antsy with the need for answers.

"I feel like I got bucked," Carla said, her voice hoarse and dry. "I haven't felt like this since..." She trailed off, not bothering to finish her sentence.

Gwen moved closer and lifted her mother's hand. "We'll get through this. We always do."

Her mother's smile was drawn and tired, but it was perfect in its authenticity. For the first time in years, the love Gwen held for her mother grew. Maybe it wasn't wrong to hope for better days.

"How are you doing?" her mother asked.

Gwen smiled. "Better. We're close to finding the person who tried to hurt you, but we need to ask you some questions. Okay?" She motioned to Wyatt.

Carla nodded, her motion stiff. "I don't know how much help I'll be."

Gwen tried to ignore the way her stomach clenched. Everything depended on this. Wyatt took her hand and made the little circles on her skin she now loved so much. The simple action made some of her nervousness disappear.

He leaned in close so his lips nearly brushed against her ear. "It'll be okay." His warm breath cascaded down her skin and, surprisingly, considering their situation, she believed him.

Even if this didn't work and her mother was of no use, they would spend every last minute going after the person responsible for Bianca's and Monica's deaths.

"Mrs. Johansen, do you know Alli Fitzgerald?" Wyatt asked.

"Alli? As in your brother's ex-wife? Sure. She came to our ranch's Fourth of July party. Why?"

"Wait." Wyatt paused. "Don't be offended...but you've made it clear that you don't like my family. Why would my brother's ex-wife be invited to your party?"

Carla sighed and she readjusted the pink hospital blanket that was arranged around her. "I don't *hate* you, or your family."

Gwen snorted with derision. "Mom, you don't have to lie to him. It's not like you hide the fact very well."

"I don't hate them, or *you*," Carla said, looking at Wyatt. "And I certainly don't hate Alli. She wasn't even around when everything happened. It's just that, sometimes when I'm drinking..."

"Your true feelings come out?" Wyatt asked with a raised brow.

"Your family, you took the only man I ever loved from me. Your family left me alone to raise two girls and run a ranch. It was all too much. And now with Bianca gone..." A tear slipped down her mother's face. "I...I just can't get through this all by myself. It's why Alli and I became friends. She just *listened*. You know?"

"You're friends with Alli?" Wyatt's voice was filled with surprise.

"Sure. We see each other at the bars all the time."

Gwen looked over at Wyatt. She'd never heard about her mother's relationship with Alli, or anyone from the bar, before. Though, admittedly, she hadn't ever bothered to ask about her mother's nightlife.

"You hang out with her? How often?" Gwen asked.

Her mother shrugged. "I dunno. I haven't been seeing her around as much lately."

"Why not?"

"Well, ever since your sister shacked up with that Poe guy... Alli didn't take it real well."

"Alli was seeing Poe for a while," Gwen said. "Did you know?"

"Yeah, though I was one of the few. I just happened to walk in on them *making things happen* in the Dog House Bar bathroom one night. She begged me not to tell anyone."

"You saw them *together*?" Wyatt asked.

"Oh, yeah, but I ain't ever told anyone. Alli was real nice. She even gave me a bottle of vodka the other night as a thank-you for staying quiet."

"A bottle of vodka?" Wyatt's voice took on a dangerous edge. "You mean the vodka you were drinking the night you were drugged?"

Her mother's face went slack. "She...she wouldn't do something like that."

"No one else touched that bottle of vodka besides you and her," Gwen said, as a wave of exhilaration coursed through her.

They had the evidence they needed. Together, she and Wyatt could bring Alli down.

Chapter Eighteen

The next morning, the police station was nearly empty as they arrived at Wyatt's sergeant's office. It had been a surprise when Sergeant Hubbard had called and woken them up, requesting that they come see him. It had been hard to find the willpower to get out of bed after Wyatt had held Gwen in his arms all night. And thanks to everything that had been happening, as they drew nearer to his superior, Wyatt couldn't help feeling that he may have been a dead man walking.

Hubbard was sitting with his back to them, talking on the phone as they arrived.

"Thanks for coming down." Hubbard hung up the phone. "Heya, Gwen. How goes it, Wyatt?"

"I don't know. You tell us," Wyatt said.

Hubbard looked at Gwen and gave her the

soft smile he reserved for people dealing with trauma. "By the way, I'm sorry for your loss. Your sister was a real nice gal. I always liked her," Sergeant Hubbard said, motioning for them to each take a seat in front of his desk.

"Thank you," Gwen said. "It will be better once we get Alli behind bars. At least then I can rest easy, knowing she will pay for what she's done."

Hubbard looked down at the files on his desk and fiddled around with the corner of one of his manila folders. "Actually, that's why I called you to my office. I got some news."

Unless it was that they had Alli in custody deep in the bowels of the county jail, Wyatt wasn't sure he was ready for anything the man had to say.

"First, Wyatt," he said, bumping the folders into a neat pile. "I have taken you off the Alaska trip. With everything going on, now isn't a good time for you to be leaving the area."

Wyatt couldn't say he was disappointed about staying. Gwen still needed him. Yet he wasn't sure he followed Hubbard's reasoning. "What's that supposed to mean, Sarge?"

Hubbard sighed. "We found Alli's car. It

was parked about an hour north. It looks like she dropped it and made her way over the Canadian border. She's gone."

Wyatt slammed his fist down on Hubbard's desk, sending his neat pile of files scattering over the surface. "Are you kidding me? She just disappeared?"

"We notified the Feds. They're going to be on the lookout for her. For now, you need to look to your family and stay close. With Christmas just around the corner and everything else going on, Sheriff Stone and I just thought it best. She may try to contact you—especially since her daughter is still in the care of your family. In the meantime, I want you both to go back to your routines. If you can, try to keep your minds off Alli."

"How am I supposed to do that?" Gwen pressed. "She's at large. And we're in danger. What if she comes back?"

Hubbard gave Gwen a soft smile. "Why would she try to come after you now? You aren't her enemy. Now she's going to be after only one thing—flying under the radar of law enforcement."

The thought didn't comfort Wyatt, but Hubbard was right. They could only concentrate on moving forward.

Without Alli, the only closure she could have would be her budding relationship with Wyatt—and all the possibilities it held. As long as they were together, they would always be safe.

Epilogue

There were moments in life when Gwen would always look back and wonder why she had made the choices she had, and how she had ended up where she was. But right now, lying in the hayloft in Wyatt's arms, she didn't regret a single thing. Even in the cool chill of the December night, it felt good. He was hers and she was his…down to the very beating of her heart.

She looked up at the beam where their names were carved into the wood. Time had worn away the harsh, jagged edges, and the scars had faded to marks that were just as much a part of the wood as the grain itself.

Wyatt ran his fingers down the length of her naked body. Reaching her hip, he pulled a piece of hay from her and let it fall from his fingers to the ground.

"Are you okay?"

She wouldn't get over her loss for a long time, but at least something positive had come out of it—her mother had agreed to go into a rehab facility. And with things heating up with Wyatt she had something to look forward to again.

He motioned between them. "I mean, with all of *this*?"

She laughed. Not at the question, but at the thought that he would ask if she was okay lying naked in his arms. There were few places she felt at home, where everything was right in the world, but with him there was no question—she was where she was meant to be.

"I'm fine. Just thinking about everything," she said, rolling onto her back. The hay was scratchy, and she wished they had grabbed a blanket to lie down on before they had fallen into the haystack just like they used to when they were younger.

It was almost surreal to be back in the same place she had been a decade before. "What are you thinking about?" he asked.

She traced her fingertips over the little line of hair that rested just below his navel. It felt good to feel all of him, to take the time to get to know his body. He had all of her heart, and she had his; it was only right that she would have all of his body too.

"I don't know," she lied. "I guess I was just thinking about..." She struggled to come up with a plausible thing that didn't involve his naked body or the love she felt. "I guess I was thinking about the holidays."

"You were thinking about Christmas? Really?" He cocked his head and gave her a playful grin.

In truth, she hadn't really been thinking about Christmas. All she could think about was the way it felt to be with him—and how much she loved him.

She nodded. "Sure."

"Well, you're coming here," he said it like it was a statement rather than a request.

"Is that right?" she teased. "If you weren't aware, I have plans on Christmas."

He sat up and grabbed his pants, pulling them on over his nakedness. "You can come to my parents'. My brothers will all be there. It will be amazing. You'll love it. Besides... you'll have to show everyone the present I got you."

"The present?" she asked, perching up on her arms. "What present?"

He reached into the pocket of his pants. "This one," he said, extending his hand. In the center of his palm was a simple gold band. He picked it up and lifted it for her to see. "Gwen Johansen, I've loved you since I was sixteen years old. I've always loved you. Nothing has ever changed. I don't want to spend another single day without you. Will you marry me?"

She sat up and wrapped her hands around his neck so violently that he had to grip the ring in his hand to keep from dropping it.

"Yes. I love you too. Yes." She buried her face in his neck, nearly forgetting about the ring in his hand.

As lovely as the band was, it was nothing compared to the beautiful feeling of being loved by him—the man who had always filled her dreams and who would now become her reality.

No matter what the future would bring, or what would happen with Alli, they would always have each other.

From this Christmas on, she would have the one gift that she'd always wanted—his love.

* * * * *

Get 2 Free Books,
Plus 2 Free Gifts—
just for trying the Reader Service!